Sergeant of the Guard: The Road in Iraq

Sergeant of the Guard: The Road in Iraq

R. Morgan Crihfield

Published by The War Writers' Campaign, Inc.
PO Box 3811
Parker, Colorado

ISBN-978-0692413036

Library of Congress Control Number: 2015936744

Cover Art: © 2015 R. Morgan Crihfield, Edited by Robin Spielberger
Cover Design: By Erin Kennedy
Author Photo: By Carla Blanchard www.blanchardportraits.com

All proceeds of this literary work go to The War Writers' Campaign, Inc. and/or any charitable cause The War Writers' Campaign, Inc. deems to distribute.

For my wife Amanda, who was there for every step.

Special Thanks to:

War Writers' Campaign
Iraq & Afghanistan Veterans of America
Jessica Bass
Jamie Dick
Geoffrey Freeman
Steve Gomez
Robert D. Hudson
Scott Nelles
Tom Strong
Eric T. Wallig
Centaur 26

Sergeant of the Guard: The Road in Iraq

"Time seemed to slip into slow motion as I saw what seemed like a shooting star headed right at me. The sound was surreal, like a deck of cards being hard shuffled and amplified through a wall of speakers, with almost a whirring or grinding sound. I remember not even thinking I was in danger, just wondering what the hell I was seeing. Time dripped like molasses. The only way I can describe it is as "time expansion" or lengthening of the time between moments. It was heading directly at me, and then seemed to shift to my right at the last moment.

It hit the ground and exploded.

It was deafening for an instant; then it sounded like I fell in a pool of water as if my ears just turned themselves down. I realized I had hit the ground. I was in shock. It was chaos. Smoke and dust filled the air all around me and I was genuinely scared because the explosion was very close and I did not know what to do. I was expecting more incoming any instant. I stood on a slight elevation next to a low ground before the blast walls protecting the CHUs and the rocket struck to the 5 o'clock of where I was just standing; beyond 30-40 meters. The whole area behind me was smoke and dust and I could not really hear or see that direction. Time was dripping away as my mind struggled to start working again."

-Sergeant of the Guard: The Road in Iraq

Preface

I wrote this book with one primary goal in mind: to tell the story of my war in Iraq. I would recommend this book for someone considering a career in the military, as I have pushed myself to be as honest as possible about the actual reality of service. This is information you will not get from a recruiter or website. This book can also be useful to a family member, medical care provider, or professional who wishes to work with the military population as it will provide valuable insight regarding the pressures of deployment, combat, and the challenges of coming home.

I will not use the actual names of any of the soldiers involved, nor any identifying information that could be considered sensitive or a risk to operational security.

These are the events from my perspective to the absolute best of my memory and journal entries. I spoke with and had other soldiers from my platoon review this book in order to ensure the most accurate picture possible. This is the story of a deployment in support of Operation Iraqi Freedom, with all the internal pressures, banalities, and details that are usually left out in traditional war stories. These details are crucial to understanding the challenges our veterans face when coming home.

I've found the best insights into war come from the accounts by the people on the ground. Whether those accounts depict trench warfare in World War I, the boredom of a sniper in the first Gulf War, or the realities of this Iraq war—we can learn best from the people who actually lived it. Historians look at the big picture and sometimes ignore the perspective on the ground.

The opinions expressed in this book are mine and mine alone and do not reflect that of the United States Army, the Texas Army National Guard, or any other organization.

Table of Contents

Chapter 1:

Agony, Misery, & Heartbreak: Army Basic Training at Fort Knox

What the hell have I done?

I imagine that countless Army recruits have asked themselves this as they arrived for processing at Fort Knox.

The sign on the main gate read: "Welcome to the Army."

Oh, Hell.

At approximately 11 pm—or 2300 as I will later learn—the bus grinds to a stop and the chatter of nervous recruits turns to silence. The bus door opens, and then we see it. The "brown round" campaign hat of a drill sergeant bobs forward, and a drill sergeant steps onto the bus. Surprisingly, he doesn't yell. The drill sergeant explains that we will "un-ass" the bus and line up in ranks of no more than 12 on the line outside. He moves like a machine, and can be heard clearly even though it seems like he is talking under his breath. He stands slightly too close to you when he speaks, and his eyes bore right through you.

He has us pile our gear "on-line and in-order quickly," then we speed walk to the chow hall. It is the unnatural ability of a drill sergeant to walk at the pace of a jog without seeming to exert any effort at all.

I was a smoker at the time, and had not had a cigarette for the better part of 12 hours by this point. I was in full nicotine withdrawal in an exceptionally stressful situation. Standing in the chow hall, we were instructed to stand directly behind the person in front of us at "parade rest," in which your feet are shoulder width apart with hands formally clasped behind you. When the line moved forward, we were instructed to stand at "attention" in which you stand straight with hands forming a natural line straight down, chest out, eyes forward and always stepping off with the left foot until the line stopped again. Then it was back to parade rest. I remember thinking that no one else I knew was standing in this eerily quiet chow hall in perfect silence, stepping forward inches at a time. I was surrounded by strangers.

This was a preview for the rest of my time at Fort Knox; the most minor event was formalized by drill and ceremony with an almost obsessive attention to detail. I was given (I still see it now) a lukewarm hot dog on a piece of white bread with cold chili on top. If you have ever been in nicotine withdrawal, you can understand how nauseous this can make you. As strange as it sounds, I felt like I had to eat it, but I could not even take a bite. I would have given anything at that point to smoke a cigarette and go home. Luckily, that was not even close to an option. I was in the Army now. It felt like the decision was seeping into my pores. I could have done any number of things besides enlist. If I had taken that retail management job, I would be asleep right now and going to work by 8 am. I could have joined the Air Force or Navy. Why the hell did I join the Army?

The drill sergeant took us to an old barracks, and the processing began. A quick note about military processing: the "hurry up and wait" concept always applies. If you have ever spent any time in the military, this is a very familiar phrase. The gist is that you need to rush to grab everything you need—paperwork, gear—and have it ready no later than a certain time. You then wait an additional two or more hours with no one knowing what exactly you are waiting for. Information will filter down through the chain of command, and this will very likely be wrong. Finally, whatever was supposed to occur will happen, but not quite according to plan, should such a plan ever have existed in the first place. That being said, U.S. Army Basic Training is one of the better-organized processes in the military.

We were brought to a room where staff checked our feet to determine our foot shapes and arches. This (I had no idea about this at the time) determined what type of running shoes we needed. I was damn near flat footed and needed motion control shoes, which forced my foot to stride properly while running.

Marched out into the hallway, we were given one minute, with a very loud countdown, to strip out of our civilian clothes and into Army Physical Training Gear (PTs). I suddenly forgot how shoe laces worked when the drill sergeant was screaming at me. Our uniform for the first few days was an Army PT shirt, PT shorts, knee-high green boot socks, and a pistol belt with a canteen and poncho. We were then processed for name tapes for our uniforms and then examined for gang tattoos, among other things.

Next we were shuffled off to a large room with school style desks where we sat for the better part of two hours, just shooting the breeze amongst ourselves. The nicotine withdrawal was killing me, and my addict brain screamed for me to step outside and light up, no matter the consequence.

One of the major differences with my Basic Training compared to others was that my time at the airport was the last time I saw a female my age for about two months. This was an all-male BCT, which is rare in more modern TRADOC (Training and Doctrine Command) models.

I tried to sleep as it was about three or four in the morning, but the withdrawals kept me in misery the whole time.

Things got *real* very quickly at this point; a new drill sergeant came in and performed like what we expected out of the first drill sergeant. We were hustled off, with the new drill sergeant seeming to be everywhere all at once and in all our faces, all the time. It's amazing how intimidating the Brown Round campaign hat can be and how your blood pressure shoots up when the man who wears it is screaming in your face.

The next several hours were a blur. I remember being shuffled into the amnesty room where you can get rid of any contraband, no questions asked. I looked at my cigarettes one final time, considered lighting up, and then decided that would be a bad move on day one to single myself out. The withdrawals continued. Later in my career, one of my better friends became a drill sergeant and told me about the stuff that ended up in that room. Let your imagination work on that one, and you won't even be close. Later, another friend told me he drank a small bottle of whiskey before tossing it away. He was an alcoholic and he detoxed in Reception Battalion. At least all I had to deal with was nicotine withdrawal.

Next up was the briefing room. About 200 of us were herded into a large auditorium where the staff briefed us on our first week in Reception Battalion. I thought Basic Training had already started. Nope. This was just zero week. After the briefing, we were given the opportunity to speak with a commissioned officer about anything that we lied about or falsified to get into the Army. Flashing in my mind was any excuse to get the hell out and smoke a cigarette while waiting on the plane home. I just sat there, tired and overwhelmed. I had been up for 24 hours and the day was just starting.

I think if you asked any Soldier, they would tell you they had serious doubts about the Army after they joined. Basic Training sucks. Point Blank. Anyone who tells you otherwise is either lying, forgot what it was like, or is trying to recruit you.

We finished the briefing. I had a headache, was tired, and the day had not even started. Honestly, I was feeling pretty stupid for joining the Army, or for not joining the Air Force or Navy. I was still pretty young, and six years seemed like a damn long time until I was done with all of this.

We were waiting for something in a breezeway by the Post Exchange mini store (PX) when a sergeant told us all a story I will remember for the rest of my life, and it still holds true to me to this very day. I don't remember his name, but he was a sergeant (E-5) and not a drill sergeant, and he will have to forgive me for paraphrasing.

"Well, what do you think?" He said.

"Hooah" we bleated back with the best false motivation we could muster.

"Listen, Soldiers. This is not the Army. This is just Basic Training. We all had to go through it, but let me tell you something. I have a friend I went to school with ·back in the day, he sells insurance. He sits in an air-conditioned office, and makes more money than me and has less stress and blah blah blah. He is bored. When people ask what he does, he sells insurance. I make less money and work ten times harder, but I also jump out of helicopters with a machine gun and do the shit that normal people can never really imagine. When people ask what I do, they pay attention. I am a combat soldier and an NCO and have been in the Army for years now and am learning new stuff every single day. How many people in their thirties can run five miles in boots? This may sound cheesy, and you don't get it yet: but you are all my brothers. I would do anything for you. I'm going to break your ass down and scream at you and make your life suck, but when it's over; there is nothing I won't do for you. I will never leave you behind, and I will kill anything that threatens you without hesitation. The Army is a great place to be. Just get through today, then tomorrow, and then go from there. If it were easy, everyone would do it."

"HOOAH, SERGEANT!" we echoed back, actually meaning it.

That whole day without sleep was a series of rooms, paperwork, being sized for uniforms, eye exams—everything was mostly a blur.

We had prior service Army and Air Force guys bunked in with us at first. There was a program during this time called Blue to Green, where separating Air Force personnel could switch over to the Army instead of being separated. If they chose that route, they had to go through a mini four week Basic Training. The prior service Army guys were pretty cool and gave us a ton of advice until they moved on. We were basically three groups: the airmen/prior service, the soldiers waiting on Cavalry Scout One Station Unit Training (OSUT), and those of us there for Basic Training.

Since I got there in what was known as the "Summer Surge," there were a damn lot of us. We did all kinds of cleaning and "fireguard," which is sitting in a chair and trying to stay awake, or patrolling empty barracks. We had to stand at parade rest and sound off with "AT EASE, MAKE WAY" when an NCO walked by and call "ATTENTION" when an officer entered the building. Honestly, I don't remember a majority of the details, but I know we got our uniforms and looked like a wet bag of potatoes, or kids wearing Dad's uniform until the drill sergeants "squared us away," a phrase meaning fixing or correcting the error of another soldier.

We also got "smoked" quite a few times. The drill sergeant tells you to do push-ups or other strenuous exercises, or to "Drop" or "Beat your Face," also meaning push-ups. There was a drill sergeant with a bullhorn in the chow hall or "DFAC" meaning dining area, who counted down our time to eat. Usually less than two minutes. You can learn to eat a lot in two minutes, it turns out.

No matter what we were doing, we were herded through like cattle harassed by the drill sergeant sheepdogs. The stress level was high and continuous. A friend of mine once said: "Just do whatever it takes to get back in your bunk at the end of the day, and stay off the radar." Sound advice.

I have to make a note about Fort Knox, Kentucky in summer. It's unbelievably hot and humid. There is rarely air conditioning in any buildings outside of the chow hall, barracks, and church. So wherever you are, you are sweating. When being issued equipment, you are sweating. When shining boots, you are sweating. You are packed together like cattle and sweating. You are not allowed to wear sunglasses, so you are blinded when standing in formation and sweat is stinging your eyes. You do not touch your face or move your arms when at attention or parade rest, so you just drip sweat. When wearing BDUs or Battle Dress Uniform you have "summers" and "winters" describing how cool the cloth is. The shined boots and BDUs have given way to at least 3 other uniforms since I joined, but the desert boots breathe way better than the old Gore-Tex leather boots. So in addition to everything else sweating, your feet are sweating and wet the whole time.

After about 2 weeks of this, Basic Training finally began. We had all of our medical exams complete and were issued our equipment. We were assigned to our Basic Training groups. The worst thing was waiting. We knew it was going to be any day. We just did not know when. Finally, we were told to gather our equipment and wait in a room. My whole Basic Training company was sitting in this hot and humid room sweating and sitting on our duffel bags. Then they told us to stand up and grab our bags. So it began.

They marched us double time to an open area several blocks away between two brown and tan cinderblock barracks buildings. Painted on the ground were outlines of footprints with numbers. Then we saw our first shark attack. The instant stress and fear a drill sergeant can cause is damn near magic. They were calling out our names all at once and assigning us to platoons. It was impossible to hear your name or know where you were supposed to be standing in the swarm of screaming drill sergeants.

Some Examples:

"You had better unfuck yourself quickly!"

"What are you staring at!?"

"What is your problem?!"

"Are you incapable of following simple instructions? Am I not asking you kindly enough?!"

"I bet you want to go home! That's not my problem! You are my problem! I will solve my problem"

"You know I own you right? When's the last time another man owned you? You are now my personal project!"

"What's your name? I will see you every day! You messed up, Private!"

My personal favorite I heard: "Dear Lord, tell me you are not crying! Al Qaeda had better not use pointed words or yell or we are all fucked".

After we were divided up, I found myself in First Platoon "Bushmasters." There were about 50 people per platoon and three platoons. The shark attacked continued and the bad drill began! We were to line up our military and civilian bags. Of course this took several attempts and we got smoked between each try, intensifying the stress and helplessness. Over and over again we screamed "Attention to detail, teamwork is key!"

We screamed out the cadence of exercise in a pit filled with dirt and sawdust in the center of the courtyard. This went on for God knows how long, but I could not do even one more push-up and my arms and legs were giving out and shaking from muscle failure. Finally, it was getting dark and we were told to grab our bags and head into the barracks.

Then it happened.

We were pouring up the stairs over the screaming of the drill sergeants and my right foot was caught in a pothole/cement ridge and twisted up and to the right with the weight of all my equipment on my back. It hurt. *It hurt* does not quite cover it. It was agony. And the cattle behind me propelled me forward and up the stairs. When we reached the top of the stairs, we were assigned bunks and told to dump our gear for another "shakedown." Basically making sure we had all of our equipment and no contraband. Anything we were not supposed to have was stuffed in our civilian bags and locked away until the end of Basic Training. The shark attack continued.

"Where the fuck are you from, Private?" snarled the drill sergeant.

"Vermont, Drill Sergeant!"

"Did you join the Army to make up for that?"

"(silence)"

"Did you not understand the question? Are you going to have a problem answering my questions? Do you have somewhere you would rather be?"

"Yes... No... I don't understand the question, drill sergeant!"

"Of course you don't. Don't worry, Private. I will help you."

The drill sergeant turned to me. "Where are you from? Why are you a Specialist?"

"Texas, drill sergeant! I have a degree, drill sergeant!" I yelled, not daring to look anywhere but straight ahead.

"Oh good. Another college boy. At least you are from Texas, some hope for you there at least. What is this?" he snarled through clenched teeth, pointing at a book I had brought with me.

"A book, drill sergeant!"

"Well, I can see that, dumbfuck. Did you think you would have some lazy Sundays reading?" He seemed amused at this point as he threw the book over his shoulder across the room.

I was of course just waiting for it all to be over for the day. It wasn't, of course. It was a long damn night. I pulled fireguard around 2 am or so with my bunkmate, a really cool guy named Chris. I woke to my foot being swollen. Turns out later I had two fractures in the foot. The clinic and drill sergeants said I could be put back in medical holding (reception) until it was healed or keep going and wrap it in a rigid brace. I would be on crutches for two weeks then have to wear the brace the rest of the time in Basic.

I really doubted I could make it, and even talked with the Chaplin about it. He said, "What else of worth could you possibly be doing other than this?" This was a moment where the drill sergeant was quite honest and told me that he would let me keep going if I would just suck it up and move forward. Done and done. I would never want to relive that first week or so after waiting in medical holding for another several weeks, but I have to be honest and say I had a real weak moment. I saw a lot of the other guys really question their decision, and three or four guys did anything they could to get kicked out or quit. Two guys in another platoon were suicidal and one attempted to hang himself with boot laces.

...

I will save you a detailed account of my entire time in Basic Training because it's a common experience to every soldier. It was 12-14 weeks long (depending on reception time) with only about 10 weeks being actual Basic Training.

Your standard day at Basic Training: wake up around 4 am immediately followed by Physical Training (PT). I usually got up 15 minutes prior so I could shave without waiting on a sink. A good tip at Basic is to bring a tough, durable digital watch like a G-Shock or Casio Iron Man so you can set alarms and reminders. PT usually consisted of "Run" days where we would perform running drills like wind sprints or long runs of three to five miles. Our "Burn" days included calisthenics and muscle building "smoke" sessions. My favorite was "Combatives" which was basically the military version of Brazilian Jujitsu that the Army adopted. It works really well. Get good at it and your ability to defend yourself shoots way up.

Our Battalion run was the longest I ran in Basic and they said it was 11 miles. I am not the person before Basic you would have called a runner, but they work you up and you get used to it. Another tip for PT is to make sure to stretch as much as possible before and after, and make sure to knock out as many push-ups as you can before Basic. Try to show up in somewhat decent shape. I did as many push-ups as I could before sleep every night and it helped me pass the final PT test. The final PT test was/is a two mile run at a pretty good pace, push-ups, and sit ups. I think it has changed somewhat since, but it is very challenging physically. After PT was chow which takes a while of standing in lines. Honestly, the food was quite good. God help you if you choose junk food or cake. The drill sergeant will wear you out.

After chow, you performed hygiene and barracks clean up, and then there was training until lunch time. Training covers all manner of fun stuff. A few things that come to mind are the rappel tower where you rappel down five stories, an obstacle course which is quite challenging and fun honestly, grenade/claymore/AT4 training, the gas chamber where you learn to trust your mask and that you will survive a CS attack however unpleasant, firing and maintenance of the M-16 rifle, night operations, combat life saver (medical training), and land navigation which includes compass and map reading. Basic Training

Basic is broken down into three phases: Red, White, and Blue phases. Each phase consists of 3 weeks.

Red is the hardcore phase where you learn the basics and are subject to intense stress 24/7 with little sleep. Anyone who says it wasn't too bad is either a liar or forgot what it was like. That being said, I am pretty sure that Basic Training at Fort Knox, Fort Sill, and Fort Benning was typically harder than Fort Jackson and Fort Leonard Wood, which were male/female integrated Basic Training units. I heard this first hand from those who went there, from both the male and female perspectives. Since there are very few areas of the military that are not integrated, there is no reason not to train the same way from day one. We are issued "rubber ducks" which are fake rubber rifles, which look and weigh the same as real weapons, and we learn basic drill and ceremony.

I am a pretty intelligent and self-assured guy, but Basic Training did its job in breaking me down and teaching me that I knew jack squat about the military. This process is called "stress inoculation." People are subjected to intense sustained pressure to see if they break or can't handle it physically and emotionally. If they can't hack it, which happened to a few people, they are separated. Most people, when violence happens, they freeze. Point blank. It does not matter how much kung fu you know or how great a shot you are: your nervous system seizes up. This consistent stress, learning to live and deal with pain and discomfort, mimics the conditions in combat. Like a vaccine, if your body is familiar with violence, pain, and stress, it won't freeze up and get you killed in the moment of truth.

White Phase of Basic Training is where you get some more freedom. For example, your platoon guide will march you back and forth to chow. Orders are given to your Platoon Guide and Squad Leaders and are given out from there. You still get smoked every day, it's still Basic Training, but your body and mind are starting to get used to it. You are issued real weapons and learn to maintain and fire them along with claymores (anti-infantry mines), AT4s (antitank missiles), M249 SAWs (belt fed machine gun, 5.56 mm), and 240 Bravos (belt fed machine gun, 7.62 mm). It was mostly familiarization with all other weapons other than the M-16. The bolt on my rifle gave me no end of crap as, turns out, there was insane carbon build up visible only when you break it all the way down (which we were not allowed to do). I still managed to fire pretty accurately with my rifle jamming all the time. It also made me forever obsessive-compulsive regarding my personal firearms. They are as clean and well maintained as a human being can make them. Being on that rifle range all day in the heat was brutal, but it was the first time I really enjoyed myself in basic.

Blue Phase of Basic puts the pieces together with a final physical fitness test, and Field Training Exercises (FTX). This is pretty brutal, honestly. The final FTX was serious, with around-the-clock war games and guard duty, as well as any number of challenging and long-running tasks. Low crawling under live fire, 24-hour per day guard, MOUT exercises (Military Operations in Urban Terrain) like clearing buildings, and ungodly road marches are a few examples of this phase of Basic.

At the end of Blue Phase, and with over 48 hours without any real sleep, came our final test. Seeing Fort Knox down the mountain through the smoke in the early morning, I knew it was finally over. Without waxing too eloquent, getting through Basic is not some impossible task. Most people will do just fine and be better for it on the other side. It also links you with every other service member because we are the only ones who really know how bad it sucks.

Day one of Basic.

Senior Drill Sergeant Durant pulled a bed out to the center of the floor and taught us how to make our racks with hospital corners. He was a 5'10, stocky, Hispanic sergeant first class (E-7) and the senior drill sergeant in the Company. This was his last rotation as a drill sergeant. He was genuinely intimidating, yet fair minded. Not sure I ever really saw him smile. This is the one I remember more than the rest.

"So that is how you do it. That is the standard. That is how it will be done. Do you understand?" as he finished the demonstration.

"YES DRILL SERGEANT!"

"Here is what you need to know about Basic Training, you will always refer to me and the other drill sergeants as drill sergeant and nothing else. You will go to war. We are at war and you will be going. I don't want to hear about what the recruiter said; he is not here. He is a liar. It does not matter what your MOS is, it does not matter what your unit does. You will go to war and you will carry a rifle. You will be called upon to kick in doors and kill. I will make you a killer. That is what I do. I make killers. I will teach you to kill so you don't die. So your battle buddy does not die because you are a pussy."

"YES DRILL SERGEANT!"

"Jody's got your girl. I don't want to hear about Mary Jane rotten crotch. She will not be there when you get back. She is probably fucking Jody right now. You joined the Army; no relationship will survive that transition. Here is a secret: fuck her. You don't need her. You now have money, a career, and respect. You are young. Shut up and get over it. Here is another secret, Jody is a pussy. You're going to be a killer. Now and forever. Do you understand?"

"YES DRILL SERGEANT!"

"You are one place: here. Don't worry about what is going on at home. Nothing will ever change there. Only you will change. Your pussy friends are playing video games and jerking off while you are learning to kill. You are exactly where you need to be. Pay attention to detail. Learn what we are teaching. You may need every bit of this to save your own pathetic ass one day. I will make your life unbearable, and you will be better for it. Do you understand, Bushmasters?

"YES DRILL SERGEANT!"

"Set fire guard and clean my damn bay right now. Then go to sleep because tomorrow is going to be hell."

"YES DRILL SERGEANT"

Of course I felt I was the exception. I tried to break up with my girlfriend before I shipped to Basic, but it did not stick. She was ok, but if anything was ever there, it was long since gone. We spoke on the phone when I got the chance, but that was pretty rare. About halfway through Basic, I got a letter from her. The note was pretty routine up until I read the part about her going on a date with some other dude. Guess what? HIS NAME WAS JODY! I knew the guy! It was hilarious. She stated that when we quasi broke up that I said that we could see other people if we wanted. She was right but my pride took a hit on this one. Fun fact: the term "Jody" is derived from an old blues song in World War II called *Joe the Grinder*, who slept with inmates' and soldiers' girlfriends while they were away.

Drill Sergeant Callen entered the room. We were all "toeing the line," meaning our toes were on the platoon seal in the center of the room at the foot of our racks. He was tall, at least 6'3" with full sleeve tattoos on both arms and a high and tight haircut. Of all the drill sergeants, he was the most funny and "laid back," which I assure you is a relative term. He referred to us as "bitches" and "dicks" when the captain was not around and apparently this got back to someone. We were immediately dropped into the "front leaning rest" or push-up position and smoked until the walls were sweating; push-ups, bear crawls, leg lifts, flutter kicks, and his favorite: Iron Mikes. They will smoke you until you can no longer bend your arms and you completely soak your clothes in sweat, like you just crawled out of a pool.

"So, someone in here has a problem with me calling you my bitches. Private Tong, do you have a problem with me calling you my bitches?"

"No, drill sergeant!" said the friendly recruit.

"Are you sure, Tong Song? I don't want to offend you here at U.S. Army Basic Training." DS Callen constantly referred to this soldier as Tong Song as a reference to the "Thong Song."

"Yes, Drill Sergeant. I am sure," said the smiling Tong.

"Ok, come on over here and hold onto my pocket." Private Tong promptly obliged.

"You are all my bitches; I don't care what anyone says. But you have the wrong idea about that. You seem to think that is offensive because you are all such sensitive little snowflakes. Being my bitch is a good thing. I take care of my bitches. When Privates Cass and Johnson had to go back to the range for two extra weeks, who went with you?"

"You did, Drill Sergeant," responded the Privates.

"Do you know why? Because I take care of my bitches. No one gets to fuck with my bitches but me. True, I won't always be gentle; but I won't let other drill sergeants have you because you are my property. Tong here, is mine. Don't you feel safe being my bitch?"

"I guess, Drill Sergeant," Tong said.

"Listen, Bitches. This is the Army. We curse and keep our business in the Platoon. This is a good lesson for when you reach your units. Don't send up the chain what can be handled in house. If you have a problem, lock the doors and handle it; it's nobody's business outside of the Platoon. If you send stuff up the chain, you can get a reputation. Alright bitches, go wash your nasty asses and get ready for mail call."

Thing was, he was right. It took me a while to fully grasp what he said. DS Callen on many occasions spoke with us and let us ask any question we wanted regarding the Army and our careers. Some of which undoubtedly filtered into this book. Drill sergeants are an amazing example of soldiers in the highest tradition of the U.S. Army. Every Soldier who has ever worn the uniform remembers their drill sergeants very well.

In the evening was drill sergeant time. Typically this covers any subject they feel is necessary, as well as mail call. I loved getting mail and had a supportive family and friends. You get "personal time" which includes hygiene and not much else. I wrote a letter or couple of post cards every night and it really helped keep me focused. There were no cell phones and you could call home for five minutes once per week if they got around to it. Lights out was around 10 pm and I was asleep as soon as I could manage. I only slept under my top blanket and not the sheets, so I would only have to fix the blanket in the morning. We used to get back from training and have our bunks tossed and wall lockers emptied onto the floor if we did not pay attention to detail; i.e., socks not folded correctly, sheets and blanket not tight enough.

Tips to Survive Basic:

1. *Basic starts before you actually arrive.*
If you smoke cigarettes or use tobacco of any kind, quit before you get there. Trust me. Don't make the mistake of taking a challenging experience and making it worse. Start doing push-ups now. A tip might be that before every meal, do as many push-ups as you can, concentrating on good form. Pushing your limits is the only way to get better, push until you can't push anymore. It only takes a minute and will help you immensely. Go for long jogs and start eating healthy. If you are really smart, start getting on the 4 am wakeup schedule before you arrive so your body does not have to adjust.

2. *Accept reality.*
You are in the Army. The time to have made a different decision has passed. I watched many, myself included, try to think of some way or reason to get out. There really is no way to do this. And if there is, you won't like the results. I saw guys try to kill themselves and say they lied about serious medical issues, or get injured purposefully. The best/only way out is through it. You don't want to be in Medical Hold or recycled in which you start Basic Training ALL OVER AGAIN for being dishonest. I saw this happen to a soldier who was obviously lying about something but would not admit it. Don't play games and stay off the radar.

If you manage to get out, you will regret it for the rest of your life. Every time you see a soldier in uniform or have to explain to your family that you did not make it through Basic, you will regret it. The Army has MANY flaws, but it is worth it if you take a deep breath and get through. There is always a cost to all the benefits. The costs are deployments and inconvenience and lost paperwork but at the end of the day you become a member of privileged class. I have a graduate degree with my name on it and I owe not one red cent in student loans. It also looks great in a job interview. They don't need to ask if you can handle stress or supervise others.

You signed and swore, now shut up and pay the piper.

3. Just keep running

I have struggled with my physical ability and weight most of my adult life. This is not an excuse, but I have to work out every day to be just a little overweight rather than quite a bit overweight. One of the things that scared me the most about Basic Training was running at a decent speed to pass the PT test. In hindsight, two miles seemed like a lot at the time, but once you get used to running on a regular basis, it is not that big a deal. For someone like me, who was never into sports or physical fitness, Basic was a wakeup call. If you are overweight or have that tendency, running two miles can seem overwhelming.

There have been a lot of changes to Basic Training since I graduated so long ago. First, there is no more Basic Training at Fort Knox. I find a tragedy in that, aside from maybe Fort Benning or Fort Sill, it was harder and the one of the few male only Basic Trainings left in combat arms. It's sad to me that soldiers no longer have to struggle up the damned tiny mountains that are famously known as Agony, Misery, and Heartbreak. Basic Training is meant to be damn difficult. It was a point of pride to me and my service that we trained how we fought.

Chapter 2

My Road to Becoming a Soldier

There are servicemen and women, and then there is everyone else. I understood that from a young age. When I was growing up, I watched my father put on the uniform of an Air Force officer and serve in two wars. I always held respect for those in uniform. My brother had very close friends and I watched as two of them joined the Marines and became different people. You can usually pick out a veteran in a crowd; they stand a little taller and scan a room a little more closely. They are more confident and, I believe, have better perspective on many things. Mind you, there are always exceptions to the rule, yet I think on average veterans are better Americans. Is that to say you must be a veteran to be a great American? Nope, but it helps.

I always knew I would be in the military one day. There were many factors which weighed in my decision to join. As a young man, I had a beard and long hair. Played guitar in a series of awful bands, and a few decent ones, and looked like a little hippy or metal kid. But, I was pretty sharp and probably better-read than most Americans. When planning my life, I wanted the American experience. I wanted to have served in the military and have that shadow box of medals on my wall. I wanted to have education, money, and a family. And despite every challenge I have faced in the military and how many flaws in the system I witnessed, I am a better person for having served and do not regret raising my right hand. I am connected to every other veteran throughout the course of history and understand that which cannot be known without wearing the uniform: the cost of the life we lead.

I graduated from college with a degree in psychology, naively thinking I would just walk in to being an officer. I also had some student loan debt, although far less than most kids as I worked my way through college and went after every scholarship I could get. I figured having a degree would give me instant employment making decent money because I am so darn sharp and likeable. Turns out, I kept the same jobs waiting tables and bartending and bar backing in the evenings.

So, I started calling recruiters to figure out what I needed to do to become an officer. I initially called the Air Force because that is the branch I knew better than the others. I don't know if the Air Force recruiters just are not under the same pressure—although it's probably a good bet—but I really never got a call back after several messages. Every time I went to the recruiter's office they were out for some reason. No exaggeration, I was home from Basic by the time an Air Force Officer Recruiter called me back.

I called the Air National Guard and Reserve as well and they could only offer me an enlistment as an E-3 in units in central Texas. They really did not have any enlisted mental health jobs in the Reserve, so basically I was done fishing. Without the officer information, I did not know what to do. I spoke with a Navy Recruiter briefly, but did not like the idea of being on a ship all the time. Honestly, I really never wanted to be a Marine and they certainly did not have medical or mental health jobs.

...

So there I was in a Subway sandwich shop on the main strip of my town. I had just ordered my food and I was tired from working a double shift bringing people enchiladas and booze. I had a college degree and smelled like refried beans and was broke. I did not know where I was going, but did not what to be *there*. A guy was standing in line with a slick black fitted baseball cap with the Staff Sergeant rank in yellow. To this day, I would still love to own that hat. He was in civilian clothes but was obviously military.

While I don't remember the exact conversation, I know I asked if he was in the service. He was, the Army. I had never really considered the Army; just never saw myself there. Not only that, he was a recruiter. We sat down and talked for a while. He was a laid back guy. I told him I wanted to join as an officer but was having no luck. He said he could help and asked what I thought about the Army. Honestly, I never wanted to carry a rifle and run all day, and his response was that there were different jobs in the military, although everyone goes to Basic. Then he hooked me: you can join as an officer.

I was off and running. I met with him in his office to discuss the process. One of the things that caught my attention was the possibility that I could be a recruiter's assistant following Basic Training. The whole idea being that I would have a job while waiting for OCS to kick off, where I believed I would commission as a mental health specialist officer. This active guard position would mean that I would be on active duty and work in my home town. Way better than waiting tables.

There are a few things to know about SSG Quinn. He is a decent guy, first and foremost. He caught a lot of crap that quite honestly was not his fault. He had a lot of recruits at the time for whom he was responsible until their training was complete and they were sent to their unit. That being said, he did not know the process for Officer Candidate School. Not only that, I did not even know the difference between the Army Reserve and National Guard. I honestly thought I was joining the Army Reserve.

I got screwed in my enlistment, point blank. A large portion of that being squarely my own fault. Joining as an OCS candidate, I did not get a signing bonus and had to enlist for six years. The idea being that after earning my commission, my enlistment would be null and void and my new officer obligation would begin. The most irritating thing was that I served almost two years in a maintenance unit with a medical Military Occupational Specialty or "MOS." When I asked to transfer to a medical unit, I was basically shut down. Most basic changes for my career took a lot of perseverance.

Every person who enters the military has a military service obligation (MSO) of eight years. This must be served in some combination of active, reserve, or inactive reserve time. So you can enlist active for four years, then serve four years of inactive reserve in which you just check in from time to time. During this inactive reserve time frame, you can be called up to active duty. This was happening quite a bit during 2003-2004 because we had sustained combat operations and we did not have the troop levels required. You might have also heard of a concept called "Stop Loss." This is where a command decision is made to retain you for a deployment even if your contracted enlistment is ended for the needs of the Army. To me, this is a hard reality many were not prepared for and I am glad this stopped in 2009. Hell of thing to be told to deploy again after your contract was up.

In order to join, I had to fill out a lot of paperwork and get set up to go to the Military Entrance Processing Station, or MEPS. Every person who enters any branch of the military has to go through this processing station. I stayed in a hotel in Amarillo with another recruit. He wanted to be a tanker and was a nice guy built like a pit bull. When I first enlisted the Texas Army National Guard (TXANG) was in the process of transferring from the 49th Armored Division to the 36th Infantry Division, so many units still had armored combat arms soldiers (tankers).

We were up and riding a van to the station at 3:30 am, which I used to think was inhuman. This was the first "hurry up and wait" military experience I had. Honestly, the staff at the station was quite friendly, but there were quite a few of us to sift through. The purpose of MEPS is to evaluate all the different criteria which would either keep you from enlisting, such as color blindness, injuries, or criminal records. Naked body scans, hearing tests, eye tests, and drug tests were just a few of the many things we were shuffled through in short order. There was a mix of excitement and "Oh hell what have I done?" in the recruits. This is where I signed my final contract; this is the place to ask for things to be written as a guarantee. Then I was told when and where I would be going to basic: Fort Knox, in the dead of summer. Some of the NCOs laughed among themselves, I didn't get the joke at the time. I get it now.

Chapter 3

Advanced Individual Training (AIT) & The Unit

Advanced Individual Training (AIT) in the Army is based on your chosen Military Occupational Specialty (MOS). This can range from four weeks to the better part of two years or more depending on your chosen specialty. I did not really put much thought into my MOS, which was a major mistake.

Initially I wanted to be a Mental Health Specialist (68X) due to my considerable education in this field, but was told this was not available. At some point I knew I wanted to be in the medical field, but did not want to go to AIT forever and a day since I joined a Reserve Component. I ended up choosing Patient Administration Specialist (68G), which was seven weeks of training at Fort Sam Houston. This simple choice kept me from being promoted at least one to two years later than I probably would have otherwise. This MOS is basically an administrative assistant job with a specialization in medical records. In the field, they coordinate care and medevac to what we call the "Next Level of Care." Basically, medical case managers make sure a wounded soldier is receiving what he or she needs medically to prepare them to move to a different facility.

For example, if a Soldier were wounded in Afghanistan, I would begin arrangements while they are still on the operating table "in-country." The wounded Joe would be airlifted to Kuwait on the way to Germany and then ultimately Stateside to receive the most appropriate care. In my home Guard unit, it would have been my job to keep up with my battalion's wounded soldiers in all levels of care, and to keep up with their "profiles," which means injuries which keep them from participating in certain events or actions.

I never really had the opportunity to perform my MOS outside of training. At least in the Guard, this is the case with most soldiers despite what a recruiter will tell you. Credit where credit is due, as I was leaving the Army, the training really became more MOS-specific and challenging. I really place credit on excellent NCOs and specifically the Readiness NCO of my company who really re-formed this unit into something amazing. Never underestimate the power of a solid NCO and an open-minded company commander.

I arrived at Fort Sam Houston and ended up staying in the prior service barracks for a day or so before they realized I was not "prior service," meaning soldiers who were retraining into another MOS and given more privileges and less oversight because this was not their initial training. If I chose to re-enter the Army enlisted, I could choose another MOS and attend training as prior service. I was given very little direction upon arrival other than to stand by.

When I finally arrived at the recruit barracks, I entered the drill sergeant's office. I expected what I had learned from Basic Training at Fort Knox, which was to get smoked until I could barely move. Nope, this place was really throwing me off. The drill sergeant signed me in and asked basic questions. I stood there at parade rest answering them. There was another soldier there on Charge of Quarters (CQ duty) who filled me in that this was not Basic Training and things were much more laid back. The drill sergeant told me to follow him, that I need to cut my hair before first formation, and walked me to a room in the barracks. It was going to be several weeks of "holding" before my class began and I would be with "Assassin" Platoon until assigned to a regular class.

I met my short-term roommates who were in the class before me and only had a few weeks left of training. They were very relaxed guys and told me how it was going to be in training.

Not sure what I was expecting, but this was not it.

The male barracks were only two floors while the female barracks was spread over two buildings. Males were the minority here. The next morning I met my drill sergeant who was actually friendly. The holding platoon was just sitting around and doing odd jobs like painting or lawn maintenance until the course began. I'm not sure how brain washing works, but I was suspicious of this lack of oversight and overwhelming freedom. I went and shaved my head since it was too late for a haircut and spent the rest of the night on my cell phone.

The drill sergeant noticed I was a specialist (E-4) and moved me into my own room in the barracks, which I kept during the entire course. He also gave me my Phase 5, which allowed me full freedom, including leaving post in the first week. Usually it takes about four weeks to get Phase 5. He never found a flaw in my room inspections, which happened weekly, because I slept in my sleeping bag on an empty bed in the room and kept my area clean like I was taught in Basic.

Training was outright easy; we showed up to a classroom every day for six weeks after morning PT and were done for the day after 5 pm. I spent the first weekend watching movies, smoking cigarettes, and walking around the post. I read several books out of the library during our breaks and otherwise just passed time. I was older than average and could not really relate with the younger soldiers, but got along well enough.

It was here I met a prior service guy, Corporal (CPL) Short. CPL Short was a nice guy who had left the military following the invasion and his turn in the Sandbox (Iraq). This was the first real story of PTSD I encountered, but will certainly not be my last. He told me a fascinating story of his time in the infantry, which scared the hell out of me. He and his platoon were holed up in some building, basically cut off from any real resupply when they started getting hit with Rocket Propelled Grenades (RPGs), rockets, and direct fire. He kind of described the sound of a blender before the RPG hit the wall and how they worked to hold it all together.

When he got home, he got out of the military and went back to the normal life. Only, he couldn't. He said the only time he was ever calm was when he was in uniform and around other soldiers. Otherwise he was angry and nervous most of the time. He had a hard time dealing with civilians and a short fuse with them he never had with other soldiers. Even though it was a pay cut and a guaranteed deployment on him and his family, he re-enlisted. His wife told him he needed to choose something other than infantry, so here he was. He never spoke with fear or arrogance, very down to earth about everything. It's not until I came home from Iraq that I really understood what he was trying to say.

The other prior service people were insufferable because they never did anything and felt they had something to prove. CPL Short didn't have to prove anything to anyone. He never called anyone out, but would point out when the other prior service people's stories were bull. There was an Air Force prior service that was a Sergeant First Class (E-7) and acted like he was in charge of everyone, including the drill sergeants. The drill sergeants were respectful yet you could tell they hated him too. Then there was a prior service Marine who had a world-class ego with a barely functioning mind. He was very high and mighty even though we were the same rank and insisted that people respect him for being prior service. If you have to tell people to respect you, you are doing it wrong. One of my favorite moments in this life was the ability to choke him out in combatives. Without being narcissistic, I really enjoyed out-performing and out-shooting all these jackwagon arrogant prior service people. This was a good lesson for me to be humble and honest when I became the old dog. I always made it a point to teach new soldiers instead of being dismissive or arrogant.

This was overall a pleasant experience and I got to see the Alamo, hang out with local friends at some of the bars, and see the great city of San Antonio. I graduated 3rd in my class without ANY studying or effort. I got to participate in Fiesta, which is a big deal at Fort Sam Houston where the locals come on post with rides, games, and fireworks. I enjoyed my time in AIT, which surprised me. It was over before I knew it and I was headed home again.

...

When I got home, I was expecting to get "put on orders" meaning Active Guard status where I would continue earning active duty pay to work in recruiting. Despite SSG Quinn's assurances it would happen any day, it never did. I had to get my old awful job back and pick up some part time work with a friend of mine at a sports hat retail store. Despite the crap money, I sat and read books all shift. A scene right out of Kevin Smith's Clerks; I got to be Randal the sarcastic clerk.

Things were not going well. I was broke, I hated my job and lived alone in a decent house in a declining neighborhood and was waiting for the military to issue me a Notice of Basic Eligibility

(NOBE) to start graduate school. There were not any real job prospects for my degree at the time. Life was quiet. Every day was exactly the same.

So then I texted my old friend Amanda while trying to text someone else on my phone. We texted back and forth for a while and we eventually started hanging out. She is gorgeous, and sarcastic as the day is long. I like a girl with attitude. She dated a friend of mine for several years and that was sort of odd at first when I considered dating her. Honestly, should could have been married to Chuck Manson previously and I would have still courted her. So things developed as they do and we moved in together in my rent home in a crappy neighborhood in north Texas. She was and is the best part of my story. I doubt you picked up this book to read about me being sappy, but a significant other will always be part of a story of deployment for better or for worse.

I worked as a recruiting assistant for the rest of the year. Sometimes my drill weekend would be working at gun shows or events giving out National Guard swag and answering questions of other potential recruits. Other times it would be conducting PT tests and silly PowerPoint classes with new recruits while they waited to go to Basic Training. Every now and again I would drive one of the new recruits to MEPS or the airport. One day I walked into the recruiting office and was told I was headed to my unit. My unit? I had a company? Sort of. I was told to report to the local maintenance detachment in my hometown on the next drill date.

A "detachment" in the military is a platoon or larger element that is geographically separated from the rest of the company. In this case, I was somehow assigned to a maintenance (mechanic) company in my home town. I, of course, had a medical MOS. This did not seem to be of concern to anyone. Since the unit was in my home town, I did not mind as much and did not push the issue. These days, I would have known that there was no way I was slotted either for the detachment or even the main company. I also would have known there was no way for me to get promoted without being slotted at my grade or higher. This was the result of an NCO being lazy and not wanting to mess with transferring me to the right unit, which was either in Headquarters or the Medical Company. I am being honest when I tell you no one is looking out for your career but you. There are several national mechanisms and regulations in the Active and

Reserve elements, which keep crap like this from happening. Not so in the Guard.

So I started my monthly training (drills) with a maintenance company. I did all the administrative and PowerPoint housekeeping nonsense the military loves so much. The Readiness NCO was cool, and the commander was a warrant officer who did not mess too much with the daily operations of the detachment.

Eventually a young 2nd Lieutenant named Major (amusingly) took command along with an acting first sergeant, SFC Ruiz, who had a thick accent and a pretty good sense of humor. Training improved dramatically and we accomplished quite a bit. The First Sergeant came up with some creative training, including detainee restrain and search, finding trip wires, and arm bars and hold releases, and clearing rooms. After less than a year, the whole detachment began to drive in a van to Fort Worth to drill with the rest of the battalion. It was a wake-up call in a lot of ways and I met some solid warriors who I remain friends with to this day. Hurry up and wait was in full effect, but we did get to conduct some very long annual trainings together and I got to know folks in the battalion.

It took me a while to realize I was stuck in quicksand. I was a relatively new soldier, trying to go to Professional Leader Development Course (PLDC), which is now or had recently changed to Warrior Leader Course (WLC). This is the school a soldier must go through to promote to or retain the rank of sergeant. I was told I was "on the list." It took me a while to realize that not only was there no list, but I was ineligible to promote because I was a medical MOS in a maintenance unit. There was a roster called a Unit Personnel Listing or "UPL" which had soldiers listed in units based on their MOS. If you were not listed in a slot which was your grade or higher, you would not promote to the next rank. I had been doing dozens of Army Correspondences courses in order to earn promotion points, which are listed separately than my college degree. When the first promotion list came down which ranked soldiers by their MOSs, I was not even on the list.

At this point I started struggling against the quicksand. I requested to be transferred to the Medical Company in Grand Prairie or Headquarters in Fort Worth which listed my MOS, with the HQ having a vacant, promotable slot. I was initially told this "was sent up" and should happen soon. When I followed up, they had no idea what I was talking about. It became a series of irritated NCOs who really did not want to bother with it since it had nothing to do with them or the other mountain of ill-defined tasks that were delegated to them. I quickly started becoming bitter. I felt I was going to stay the same rank my whole enlistment no matter what I did.

Finally, I went to the Army Reserve recruiter's office and got a DD 368, which is a request for conditional release allowing me to join the Army Reserve and serve in my MOS and be promoted. Knowing what I knew then, I actually had a shot of making an enlisted career out of it until I finished graduate school. I gleefully submitted a copy of the form to the company and battalion readiness NCOs. As per regulation/policy, the Guard had 180 days to give me a formal response. It was supposed to go to the unit, battalion, and brigade commanding officers, and then to Austin for formal approval.

The months went by; I checked in and was told it was on the battalion COs desk. I was an irritant, my name was mud. I do not write this as "revenge" and I imagine that is a fairly common experience in the military. Documents get lost more often than they arrive at their destination, especially in the Guard. I write this so people know what you are dealing with when you join. To this day, there are solid soldiers with two or more combat deployments that are still specialists (E4) and some truly incompetent ass kissers who are staff sergeants or higher. That is life in the military. My active duty friends say it is no different with their component.

"I need to talk to you guys for a second," said LT Major.

We put out our cigarettes and headed into the barracks and took our seats during a long drill weekend at Camp Swift. Something was up. LT Major was a solid officer and very honest and real with us. "I want to let you know that the orders have come down. We are deploying to Iraq," he said simply.

I felt my blood pressure spike. I had been so focused on shifting to the Reserves it did not occur to me that we would be deploying so soon. It had been less than three years since the brigade returned from Iraq and we thought it would be on the fourth year that we would be gearing back up.

"Gentlemen, it's going to be a long road. I will not lie to you, I have been in the briefings and this is a done deal. I have heard a few things, but nothing solid. I think we will be force protection; kind of like gate and tower guards with artillery and cavalry battalions doing the combat operations. There will probably be some maintenance jobs but that is not our mission."

My head was spinning. After we were dismissed, I went outside and called Amanda. I chain smoked cigarettes and honestly felt scared and angry. Working at Brook Army Medical Center, the Fort Sam Houston main hospital, I saw soldiers coming back from the sandbox missing limbs and burned so badly you could barely recognize them from their ID card pictures. Then there was the fact I knew full well that there was no chance I would promote even while deployed. I had dropped school twice due to surprise or disaster assignments and was finally back in school, and I would be dropping a third time. I spoke with everyone about what was around the corner and simply had to process what was happening to me. For some soldiers this did not bother them one bit, while others were on their way out and were hoping not to be "stop lossed," or not released at the end of enlistment.

The next drill I had asked my LT to check where I was on the form 368 release request for me to go to the Reserves. Another soldier submitted his form and was at his new unit within six weeks, while I could not even get a straight answer. I knew full well I would deploy with the Reserves as well, but at least I had the possibility to promote. He asked me if I had a degree because the battalion CO was looking for enlisted persons with education. Not long after, I met with the battalion commanding officer. She was a lieutenant colonel who was later promoted up to brigadier general at Division. She was cordial, intelligent, and very political. For some reason, I was nervous as hell. I knew this meeting was going to have an unbelievable impact on my future.

She introduced herself and asked quite simply why I wanted to leave. I stated that I had submitted this paperwork prior to knowing about the deployment and would like it honored so I could pursue promotion and a career. She asked what I thought about being direct commissioned as an officer. This struck me like a ton of bricks. I had long since stopped thinking about commissioning, especially in this branch and thought direct commission was for specific legal and medical degrees. She said that they were deploying and were very short on officers and that I would be direct commissioned as a "Science Officer." We had a long conversation and I agreed to rescind my request for release if I could be transferred to headquarters or the medical company so I could have the ability to promote. I would consider with my family whether to accept the direct commission after reviewing what that would entail. I was even offered an opportunity to work as a social worker for the battalion rear detachment.

I spoke with LT Major afterwards and he had some insight to share. I carry this with me to this day, because it was an accurate rendering of my own role in my current situation. He was a straight shooter, which was refreshing.

"Listen, let me tell you what others are going to say about this situation and how it will be viewed. I understand where you are coming from, but you already have a degree and people are going to wonder why am I deploying when he isn't? This is what we signed up for, you are a good soldier and I would rather have you with us overseas. You can see things others don't really ever see. You want to be in mental health? How else will you understand another soldier without deploying? While you have a good opportunity here, who knows how all of this will shake out?"

He was absolutely right. He was savvier to the reality of the Guard's inner workings and probably knew I just got hustled. Remember this about your career: no one is looking out for your career but you.

...

I was told in final formation by my first sergeant that I was being transferred to Charlie Company. This first sergeant made a point to tell me he fought against it because he wanted me to deploy with Bravo Company. He is a decent guy who later became the battalion sergeant major and advocated for the common soldiers against the ever-changing vague winds of command directives. Just like anything else, nothing is ever simple.

I called and emailed my new unit readiness NCO, SFC Saulchek, at Charlie Medical Company to let them know when I was coming and to ask what they needed from me. The transition did not go well. I found out later that this NCO did not like another soldier being assigned to his company when they were already way over strength, with several slots having three to four soldiers already assigned. He chewed my ass and hung up on me. Apparently he and the battalion CO got in a pissing contest about me and he lost. It boggles the mind it took this level of headache for something so simple. Of course, nothing else in my conversation with the battalion CO was honored.

I have a lot of respect for SFC Saulchek for the loyalty he engendered from his soldiers despite him being subtle as a sledgehammer. He did not care for me whatsoever, but treated me fairly despite his opinion. He promoted and deployed early with a "Dustoff" or medevac unit, which are helicopters that picked up wounded wherever they may be. His replacement was a recently promoted sergeant (E-5) who I came pretty close to giving a beating. I'm not aggressive nor a "tough guy" but he was out-right disrespectful to me when I was speaking with a social work officer about her career path. He said I could go back to school when he said so. I walked away with my fists clenched and kicked over a chair on my way out of the office to the smoke pit. I learned other medics thought that was funny and they did not care much for the guy either; that he was just showing off because he was a new sergeant.

From then on, I met with and served with the finest soldier-medics this military has to offer. Charlie will always be my home unit. I was about halfway through my enlistment and had finally found that home. With very few exceptions, Charlie Company was squared the hell away. Training was serious and the NCO Corp was solid. Word was that since ours was not a medical mission, the company would be divided up among the other units. Thankfully, that was not the case. Charlie Company was going to war, but as fighters—not medics.

Chapter 4

Operation Iraqi Freedom

September 11, 2001. I woke up, rolled out of bed, and walked right into the shower. I had long hair and a scruffy face and put on my normal uniform: jeans, boots, and a t-shirt. I lit up a cigarette while drinking my coffee on the way to my Abnormal Psychology class. I drove to Midwestern State University in my 1996 Honda Civic hatchback. It was maroon, with torn seats and an interior that was literally falling apart. I was 20 years old. The radio was playing classic rock when the news came over that a plane had hit a building in New York. Not much more was known yet.

I did not think much of it. For some reason, I figured it was a single seat prop plane. I don't know why or how something like that could happen, but I figured there were going to be a few deaths and they would report it was some crazy guy or a freak accident like happens all over America every day. I headed into class and sat down, pulled out my book *Better Than Life* by Grant Naylor, who wrote the British *Red Dwarf* series. I grew up over in England as an Air Force military brat and developed a taste for British humor. The rest of the class filed in and took their seats. Random conversations and noise filled the room. Dr. Cottington walked in with a serious look on his face as he wheeled in a television.

Something was wrong.

"Another plane has hit the World Trade Center... Something is happening. They are saying it was an attack..."

He just stood there for a moment, and then turned on the television.

We sat and watched the smoke billow out of the wounded north tower. Then the unthinkable happened. They warned about graphic imagery and language, and then showed footage of a second large passenger plane hitting the south tower. It was the most horrific thing I had ever seen. Watching a second plane full of terrified people die a violent death sent my mind into shock, just like the rest of America in that moment.

Not long after, another plane hit the Pentagon. We were under attack. We were at war. We just did not know with whom yet.

These days, I work with adults and soldiers who were too young to remember this. To them, it's academic. They don't remember the level of freedom and anonymity we had that we lost along the way because we were scared. It's now just something covered in social studies class, yet that attitude completely misses the point. We gave away our constitutional rights with both hands for the illusion of security.

I doubt Bin Laden ever expected this attack to be as successful as it was. It changed America forever. Before this, we lived in a somewhat-free American world. Then our safety was gone, we were vulnerable. We had no idea how many more planes would be hitting how many more buildings. We put soldiers in subways and waited to see how our leaders would react. We were all wounded, and very angry. And that anger had to go somewhere.

In order to explain the basics of the Operation Iraqi Freedom, there are terms that must be clarified and people to identify.

1. Osama Bin Laden: A Saudi Arabian founder of al-Qaeda, of the Sunni Branch of Islam. Fought with the Mujahedeen against the Soviets in Afghanistan. Declared holy war against the U.S. and other Western Countries and wished for strict adherence to Islamic Law. Involved in, if not directly responsible for, a number of violent attacks, including bombings of U.S. embassies. He was killed in Abbottabad, Pakistan by U.S. Special Forces on May 2nd, 2011.

2. al-Qaeda: A Sunni militant Islamist group responsible for numerous violent attacks against non-Sunnis, westerners and their countries, and other political targets. They wish for a return to Islamic Law and the destruction of Israel.

3. Taliban: Islamic fundamentalist movement in Afghanistan known for brutal treatment of women, children, and strict brutal killings and punishment for anything seen as offensive under Sharia Law. Has its roots in the U.S.-funded and trained Mujahedeen. This political movement held sway in Afghanistan following Soviet withdrawal and remained during 9/11 in support of al-Qaeda. Following their overthrow, they became an insurgency, which remains in Afghanistan.

4. Sunni Muslim: The largest branch of Islam. Something along the lines of 85-90% of the world's Muslim population belongs to this group.[1] The major split between Sunni and Shia occurred following the death of Muhammad, prophet of Allah, and the argument over his proper successor. Sunni were the ruling people group in Iraq, despite being a much smaller portion of the population. Shia were treated as second-class citizens and were brutally oppressed, along with the Kurds.

5. Shia Muslim: Comprise about 10-15% of the Muslim population of the world. Brutally oppressed by the Sunni under Saddam Hussein. The countries of Iran, Iraq, and Bahrain are predominantly Shia in population. Reprisals and old debts broke out following the removal of Saddam from power, and the current government in Iraq is strongly Shia.

6. Muqtada al-Sadr: A Shia Cleric and political leader who called for withdrawal of all U.S. Forces in Iraq and many times called for violence and killing of American soldiers during my deployment there. Continues to be a serious political power player in the country, and moves back and forth between Iraq and Iran.

7. Kurds: Ethnic and religious subgroup with distinctive culture and language, accounting of about 15% of Iraq's population. Mainly in the Northern, oil rich regions of Iraq, the Kurdish people were brutally oppressed by Saddam in

---

[1] "Sunnis and Shia: Islam's ancient schism," BBC, http://www.bbc.com/news/world-middle-east-16047709.

the late 80's, when he butchered over 100,000 ethnic Kurds, including the world's deadliest poison gas attack which killed over 5,000 Kurds.[2] They have an autonomous territory in the north of Iraq and are mostly friendly towards American troops. I have seen blonde Kurds with blue eyes, very distinctive in appearance from the typical Iraqi population.

Following the successful early operations in Afghanistan, the Bush Administration turned its attention toward Iraq. The media spoke of U.S. Intelligence Agencies beginning to pressure Iraq to permit inspections of its chemical facilities. The Bush administration claimed it possessed intelligence pointing toward a connection between Saddam Hussein and 9/11, as well as the now-infamous Weapons of Mass Destruction (WMDs), including chemical weapons and yellow cake uranium.

I, like many, was pretty skeptical of this simply because of the history the former Bush administration had with Iraq with the Gulf War. But then I saw Colin Powell plead the case to the United Nations. I had a lot of faith in Colin Powell at the time, and if he thought that there was a connection, or that Iraq was planning on using chemical weapons or giving them to our enemies, then perhaps we needed to respond. They played the footage from Saddam's poison gas strike on the Kurds, and it was a convincing case. My mistake in this time frame was that I was certain no intelligence agency would make a call like this without being absolutely certain there was a clear threat. I underestimated the pressure Rumsfeld and Cheney put forth to make this war happen. I despised Donald Rumsfeld for many of his comments at the time, and to this day still baffled by their arrogance and negligence, which cost American lives.

In 2003, the United Nations weapons inspectors were withdrawn and the invasion began. The United States, United Kingdom, Australia, and other coalition nations conducted a brutal, swift, and ultimately successful push to remove Saddam and his Ba'athist party in about a month's time. Prior to the invasion, General Eric Shinseki accurately stated to the Armed Forces Committee there would need to be several hundred thousand troops to occupy Iraq and keep some semblance of order following the invasion. Rumsfeld, Cheney, and

---

[2] "Al-Anfal and the Genocide of Iraqi Kurds, 1988" Center for the Study of Genocide and Human Rights, Rutgers, http://www.ncas.rutgers.edu/center-study-genocide-conflict-resolution-and-human-rights/al-anfal-and-genocide-iraqi-kurds-1988.

Wolfowitz of course dismissed his expert opinion out of hand and things spiraled following the invasion. Early on, the Iraqi people were welcoming of our troops and were not entirely sure what would happen next. The old iron hand of Saddam, which held the country together, was gone, and nothing was in place to fill the vacuum.

In 2004, sectarian violence ignited in Iraq. The Sunni had long been used to holding sway in Iraq and bristled at suddenly being on equal footing with the Shia. With Saddam gone, all religious differences came to a head, and old debts were paid in blood. Revenge killings and age-old tribal grudges came due while the population began to loot without military or police in place. Under the leadership of Mutada al-Sadr, a Shia force known as the Mahdi Army ignited a wave of violence against American and coalition forces in the south, while a bloody major military offensive kicked off with the ambush and killing of Black Water mercenaries in Fallujah. Insurgents and weapons poured into the country from everywhere, especially Iran, for the opportunity to kill American Soldiers. We had nowhere near the level of troops or equipment to combat this wave, and the use and effectiveness of the IED came to the forefront. Prisoner humiliation and torture in Abu Ghraib set back Middle East relations, and led to worldwide outrage and local retaliation toward American forces.

...

In Basic Training in Fort Knox, a young Specialist Crihfield was shown the offensive in Fallujah on television by his drill sergeant.

I watched young men with patchwork equipment shot to pieces and losing limbs in vicious house-to-house fighting. Our drill sergeant showed us footage he took himself during the invasion, as well as a video of a Russian soldier being decapitated with a knife by Chechens in Afghanistan. We watched every bloody death he could show us. He wanted us to see what could happen. What *would* happen.

"Pay attention to what you will learn here," he told us. "It will save your life. See that Russian? He surrendered. And now he is on YouTube getting his head sawed off by these hadji pieces of shit. Never surrender, fire every last round you have, then beat them to death with the rifle, then use your knife, then your hands. Gouge out their eyes and bite off anything you can get your teeth in. If you are going to die, then make them kill you there. It will be much better than the alternative."

Through 2005, American forces continued to face mounting casualties and manning issues. Both the active duty Army and National Guard missed their recruiting efforts by a wide margin, and the all-volunteer military was stretched thin with deployment extensions and less than one year at home before deployment back to combat. Visible anti-war efforts began in earnest at home with Cindy Sheehan, who had lost her son in Iraq, camping outside of the Bush Ranch. Democrats' criticism became increasingly apparent and gained political traction, eventually leading the way for sweeping elections of Democrats into the House and Senate.

In 2006, sectarian violence increased with the bombing of an important Shia shrine, leading to retaliation against Sunni insurgents. The Washington Post broke the story that an independent commission confirmed that there was neither WMDs nor credible intelligence to justify the war. This led to increased American frustration with the stalled progress and apparent lack of a cohesive plan. Prime Minister Maliki, elected to a splintered government, began to create some infrastructure, and pressed for a U.S. troop withdrawal timeline. The Army and Marine Corps initiated a drastic increase of "Stop Loss," forcing soldiers and Marines to stay beyond the end of their enlistments. American IED casualties reached an all-time high, while Army generals declared Iraq in a state of civil war. Public opinion overwhelmingly leaned toward ending the war and returning the troops home. The first massive increase in the military diagnosis of PTSD, depression, and substance abuse as well as an increase in divorce rates became apparent. Saddam Hussein was sentenced to death by hanging.

In 2007, the civilian and military approval ratings reached an all-time low for the Bush administration's handling of the war. The administration announced an escalation, which was opposed in the House. U.S. Marine General Pace announced that there was not enough equipment in Iraq and armor for additional troops, while civilian and American causalities further increased. Scandal hit as Walter Reed medical facilities were underfunded, and filthy treatment for wounded soldiers and service members was exposed.

The surge of 20,000 more troops was formally announced, leading to the call up of 12,000 National Guard soldiers, including my Brigade Combat Team.

In 2008, General David Petraeus briefed Congress on the security gains the first of the surge troops made, but they are both "fragile and reversible." GEN Petraeus initiated an embedded soldier counter insurgency model, where instead of soldiers venturing out from well protected large bases, small company-sized units would be posted in outposts within Iraqi cities, providing security for their areas. This allowed the military to keep security gains they made, and let them respond almost immediately to enemy action in their areas. Charlie Company and CET 26 began rolling convoys to supply these operations following a spike in roadside bomb fatalities.

Political pressure built at home by presidential hopeful Senators Obama and Clinton for troop drawdown and withdrawal. The "Sons of Iraq" policy helped pay former militia members to improve security in their region instead of fighting American forces. Violence decreased for the first time since the war began in 2003. Weapons and fighters continued to pour into the country, especially from Iran, and dozens of smuggled caches of EFP IEDs were intercepted by American and coalition forces.

Amusingly, a shoe was thrown at President George Bush by an Iraqi journalist as a sign of disrespect.

In 2009, now-President Barack Obama announced a troop withdrawal time table with all forces to exit the country by December 2011. A spike in violence and car bombings and IEDs occurred as a political statement to discourage free elections. The military announced that the additional surge troops would leave Iraq by September 2009, when Charlie Company CET 26 was scheduled to return to Texas. Renewed fighting kicked off in Mosul in northern Iraq to root out Sunni and Baathist militias.

In 2010, January marked the first month in the Iraq War with no American combat deaths. Americans took a step back from combat operations and allowed Iraqi forces to conduct patrols and offensives as needed. Operation Iraqi Freedom was concluded and the announcement of Operation New Dawn began that August.

In December 2011, the last American Forces convoyed out of Iraq into Kuwait, marking the end of the Iraq War on December 18th, 2011. On November 14th, SPC David Hickman was the last U.S.

Soldier killed in Iraq. Over 20,000 Embassy staff and U.S. Marines remained in Iraq with over 5,000 private security contractors.

According to the Department of Defense website: [3]

1. 4,487 U.S. Service members were killed in Iraq, with 32,223 wounded during Operation Iraqi Freedom.
2. During Operation New Dawn: an additional 66 killed and 332 wounded.
3. 318 deaths from Coalition countries and 179 United Kingdom Soldiers killed in action.
4. Department of Defense estimates approximately 27,000 insurgents were killed in combat operations by American Forces.
5. Most estimates indicate over 100,000 civilian Iraqi deaths.

---

[3] http://www.defense.gov/

Chapter 5

Train Up

"The rest of my life is on the other side of this deployment. My life is now lived in short term goals: a quiet smoke, air conditioning, or a cup of coffee. I was jealous of the shit truck guy today. I smoked a cigarette outside after getting 3 hours of sleep and watched him listen to music and vacuum shit out of the port-a-johns, knowing he would be off work soon and not in this God forsaken place."

Journal entry, July 8, 2008

We arrived at Fort Polk Joint Readiness Training Center (JRTC) to begin our train up for the deployment. JRTC provided training that immersed a company in 24-hour, stressful, realistic events to prepare for deployment. These training centers are well off of the garrison grounds of a military base, and are meant to simulate a combat forward operating environment. These first weeks of our train-up were more or less spent scrambling from one task to another, alternating between actual assignments and training to "try to look busy." I remember completing some training around one in the morning then waiting outside to sign paperwork, knowing full well we had a 430 am wakeup call.

Deployment training is when common sense dies a lonely death. We barely had time to shower or wash clothes, and the food was barely edible. Our first sergeant ended up being SFC Ruiz, who managed to put some boot to civilian contractor ass when he heard they were being skimpy with food. We slept in a trailer with about 30 Soldiers per room. At first, our females were in the same trailer as the males, until our platoon sergeant finally convinced someone higher on the chain that was a very bad idea. During a deployment, you live right on top of one another, with about two to five feet between the aluminum and steel cots. You live out of less than two duffel bags' worth of gear. You sleep with your feet alternating with the soldier beside you to cut down on illnesses spreading in a barracks environment from coughing. This also means you had better hope the soldier next to you gives a damn about hygiene. You are not allowed to put up barriers because it's a fire hazard and reduces air circulation, which is vital in close quarters.

The rumor mill is a hellish thing in the military. You hear any variation of a dozen different rumors that have a serious effect on your life, and you have no way to know how valid any of them are. Specifically, it is hard to confirm anything because things change so quickly. A few rumors that were floating around involved how much time we'd get to spend at home before or between training events. We had a few days after our time at JRTC where we could go home before the next phase of training began, and the current rumor at the time was that leave would be cancelled. It tears your guts up finding out that you won't even get a few days off when you are working like a dog 24/7 in a high-stress environment.

Word came down from one of my staff sergeant buddies who worked in command that we would be on guard duty at Camp Taji overseas, while Bravo Company would be at Camp Victory doing the same thing. The other units would be on convoy duty, which we all knew was the truly dangerous assignment.

JRTC had us performing some impressive training, all complaints aside. We conducted weapons ranges galore: M4 (rifle), M249 SAW (5.56 mm machine gun), M240 Bravo (7.62 mm machine gun), and Mark19 (belt fed automatic grenade launcher). We conducted live fire convoy drills. JRTC had actual Iraqi-American citizens who volunteered to portray villagers in any number of scenarios to challenge you to think on your feet. We conducted some difficult road marches and a series of station-based force security training, as well as combat aid training. The training was very impressive and well thought out. There is no doubt this training saved many lives, as it taught soldiers how to react to the reality of the situation on the ground, which involves more than just combat. Diplomacy and knowing your role and mission, as well as keeping your head on a swivel, are very important skills to learn while "downrange." This training also allowed higher command to evaluate their subordinate leaders. Trust me; several people will be fired before you make it downrange.

...

In 1st Platoon, "Just the Tip" was our motto, which I am proud to say I came up with. My buddy Tom got some 7.62 rounds and drilled them out for our dog tags. When the Company was called to attention, we called out "JUST THE TIP!" which got any number of funny reactions from high ranking brass. It was also our "callback" when saluting. For example, an officer would pass, I would salute, and he would say "Arrowhead" and I would say "Just the Tip." Our platoons were later divided up somewhat, but the overall platoon remained intact for most of the deployment. We had soldiers from the original Medical Company, myself included. Other soldiers came from companies within the battalion and from a military police company in south Texas.

SFC Ruiz was our acting first sergeant, along with Major York who was the company commander. It is not normal for a major to be a company commander, but this was because the medical officers were mostly majors and lieutenant colonels. We also had a great infantry lieutenant named Ortega. Kind of a small build, but he was tough and had a sense of humor. He never sold us out that I ever heard about; although he would bump heads from time to time with one of our staff sergeants. Plus, he had the most important element: he was not weak or a coward, which I did see from time to time in the company. Our platoon sergeant was a really nice old artilleryman from south Texas named SFC Rocha who was close to retirement. He was very soft spoken and smoked like a chimney. Good NCO, but he was overwhelmed most of the time. We were lucky to have good staff sergeants, sergeants, and corporals.

The rosters, or official sign in sheets, became a running joke because there were classes we had to take several times because someone lost the roster. This happened all the damn time. Often, we were trying to look busy while the command conducted whatever administrative nonsense they did all day at the Tactical Operations

Center or "TOC." Sometimes we had to repeat training for whatever reason—even when it was complicated and costly.

For example, one of the best days I had in the military was on the M249 Squad Automatic Weapon firing range conducted by the 45th Infantry Division "Dirtybirds" of the Oklahoma Army National Guard. They were solid infantry soldiers who were supporting our operation by conducting their annual training or "AT" while running ranges or other training events.

We began by "zeroing" the machine gun by adjusting the sights to its particular shooter, and then fired bursts of three to five rounds into various paper targets. Later we engaged distant pop up targets, then onto night fire which included firing at chemical lights tied to closer targets. Expert qualifying soldiers were given a bunch of extra ammo, and we went to town. Honestly, it was amazing to burn so much ammo so quickly, however we wanted. I lit my cigarette on a red hot barrel. While this was a blast, this took from 0445 until well after midnight through Louisiana summer. Best of all, the paperwork never made it back to command. We had to go do it all over again, so then I made extra copies and kept my scores for my own record. Then, they lost it again. Seriously.

Training conducted by the JRTC cadre was actually quite advanced and relevant to our deployment. For example, we had a "shoot house" which accurately simulated an M16 range on a movie theater screen without us having to spend thousands of rounds of ammo for familiarity. There was a vehicle rollover simulator in which about 200 troops broke down into groups of four and entered a vehicle with all our gear on. A rotating frame would tip and roll, just like a real Humvee rollover accident. We then had to unbuckle ourselves and exit the vehicle. This is important because we were losing a lot of guys overseas to vehicle wrecks, especially in water.

There was a full platoon dismounted infantry tactics course which had several stations and full combat simulations which involved blank ammunition and "MILES" gear which emits a high pitched sound when you are hit by a laser. There was force protection training in which we alternated guarding gates, towers, and searching vehicles and civilians (played by actual Iraqi nationals). Other soldiers played OPFOR or "Opposing Force" to fight against us.

To me, one of the best trainings offered was "reactive fire," which was a relatively new live fire concept where a soldier patrols and has to react to targets popping up around him. Basically, it hammered into you: scan, identify, ready, fire.

Honestly, the training was top-notch and exhausting. In the Army, there is a common theme of "train as you fight." Time and again it is proven that the closer the training resembles the actual combat, threat, or mission, the better it prepares you to face real danger and react appropriately.

On the last day at Fort Polk, when everyone was packing up and resting following some difficult training, I was detailed as CQ for the better part of eight hours. I wrote in my journal because there was very little else to do, and I felt the weight of it all, which tends to press down on you when you get a chance to think. I still had over 13 months left in this deployment. This wearing reality would be my life for over the next year. The same people, the same pressure, and the looming plane ride to Iraq were all coming up. As tired as I was of the nonsense inherent in a soldier's life, it had not even really begun. There is a cloud that hangs over everything before a deployment. You can never really relax, even when at home with your loved ones, because you feel the seconds sliding away and you know the pain of leaving again is just around the corner.

The storm was on the horizon, and I looked around at my fellow soldiers and friends, wondering who was not going to make it home. And if they did—would they be the same?

...

"We drove from Fort Polk, Louisiana to Camp Bowie, Texas where hundreds of sunburned Soldiers in worn out uniforms descended on fast food and gas stations like locusts. We have been under thumb for over a month eating contracted garbage and awful tasting water. On the way to Bowie, we did not know when we would get this opportunity again and Soldiers bought out all the essentials for a Texas Soldier: Tobacco; both chew and smoke, jerky, and anything else not nailed down. We chain smoked at the stops and called our loved ones, happy to have a signal away from the swamps of Fort Polk.

When the buses pulled up we were assigned a section of a metal building stacked on top of each other once again. Ants were crawling on the bunks and the air conditioners for part of the building had given out. Of course it did."

Journal entry, June 2008

We were stacked up and miserable while rushing to and from classes, waiting to be released in less than two weeks to go home for the better part of July. It would be our last time at home. The male barracks could be a harsh environment, and we became cavemen pretty quickly. I remember playing cards with my friends when some artillery guys were wandering around our barracks. Things started to escalate rather quickly because we were of the opinion that there is no reason for them to be in our area unless they were trying to steal something. It almost became a pretty good beating for one young private who got a little too cute with one of our guys when told to be somewhere not here soon or else. I was reading on my bunk during one of our few down days before night training, and Specialist Dayton who used to be a drill sergeant back in the day had hardcore pornography playing full blast on the laptop computer for the barracks to enjoy.

A female 1st Lieutenant walked in from another company with her NCO and asked, "What exactly is that?"

To which SPC Dayton replied, "While I am not an expert, that looks to me like some chick getting balled." To which we all erupted laughing. I was in ear shot when she complained to LT Ortega who asked her what the hell she was doing in the male barracks in the first place, which was a pretty good question.

The time passed slowly. There was always some delay or another for us to get back to our home station, which for me was still two hours away from my home. We were sitting around our local drill hall, just down the road from home, burning the precious little time we had with our families stateside while waiting on a final formation to be released. I smoked cigarettes and paced, walking anxiety. Finally we were dismissed and I was driving home for the last time before Iraq.

I ached for my fiancé and spent the 4th of July on the lakefront property of a friend. I had a cold beer and watched the fireworks, completely preoccupied. The cloud was always there, I was constantly thinking about how much time was left. I was busy making sure everything was in order with my job. Many soldiers returned to find their jobs gone despite all the legal protections. I made sure Amanda would be the beneficiary of my $600,000 life insurance policy if I did not make it back. Packing and buying things I thought I needed for deployment also took some time. I could enjoy the day and the time to relax until night time, when the stress and intrusive thoughts keep me awake.

The following weekend, my friends threw me a going away pool party, which was a blast. All my friends and family were there to eat good food and have fun. I was drinking rum and coke. At least with rum, the hangover was usually not too bad and I did not want to waste time. Amanda and I had long walks around the lake where we would eventually get married. We watched movies, talked, and went out for coffee. Time flew. Before I knew it, my family came to my house to say our final goodbyes. I held it together and sent them on their way with my best so I could say goodbye to my dogs. That, for some reason, really hit home. I sat there with my dogs, getting choked up, feeling overwhelmed. I found myself wrapped up in events half a world away, and it all seemed so big.

Amanda and I drove to Grand Prairie and got a nice hotel. This would be our last few days at home station, and she did not want me to spend my nights alone. We ate at a nice restaurant when we arrived, and ran into some other soldiers who invited us to come drinking. I was not about to spend the last moments with my fiancé drunk with other soldiers I would see for the next year. We saw a movie, which was terrible, and she broke down crying in the car as we were leaving. The pressure was just so immense; it's hard to describe. We knew that this could be our last time together, period. She heard the stories I told of my time at Brook Army Medical Center, seeing horrifically burned and injured soldiers undergoing surgeries and trying to piece themselves back together. She watched the news; we were to be part of the troop "surge" into Iraq to reestablish some control as the sectarian violence escalated. It was a heavy weight we had not yet learned to carry.

This was technically a three day drill weekend before we went back to Camp Bowie in Brownwood. Despite the fact that this was the last time we had at home, we were kept late every day for no apparent reason. One day I did not get back to the hotel until 8 pm because we were doing stuff we could have been doing all day. I was very angry and bitter and desperate to spend every second I could with Amanda. My eyes opened Monday morning and I felt my stomach fall as it all settled in. We checked out of the hotel, got some coffee, and drove to the unit. We spoke somewhat and listened to music and discussed what Amanda would be doing the rest of the day in the Metroplex. Honestly, I felt sick and had a terrible sadness. Being a father as I write this now, I cannot imagine how much worse it would be to leave children behind as well.

We arrived at the unit and I checked in, and then went back to the car to spend every last moment I could with her. There were no words, just the pressure about what was about to happen. Finally, the call for formation came and I stepped out of the car and said goodbye to my partner and best friend. I tried to hold it together as I kissed her then stepped away toward the buses. She started the car and left. Then something happened that made me sick. Turns out it was just an information formation which lasted about 20 minutes, and we were back to "hurry up and wait" mode. I considered calling Amanda back, but figured that by the time she arrived we would be gone.

So I smoked cigarettes and talked with a friend I had not seen since before Basic Training, a prior service guy who served in Iraq previously. If you have ever seen the 80s wrestler, Sergeant Slaughter, that's him. Real tall with an Army mustache and shaved head, who was apparently assigned as the Battalion Commander's driver, but until then was be assigned with the rest of the fillers to Charlie Company. His name was SPC Wallander who later attended my wedding and lived in my home town. As always, we discussed what the plan was and what we both had heard; which ranged from being switched over to Afghanistan to some of our medical people being pulled over to a hospital in Balad.

I loaded my bags and took my seat on the bus. A soldier popped in a Kat Williams DVD and I was happy to put on my headphones and disappear. I let Flyleaf, Chevelle, and Alice in Chains drown out the world as the bus pulled away. The road before me seemed daunting and clear. I would never be further away from my life than this moment. There were about 400 days left in the deployment and the road already seemed so long. I knew things were going to change, I just did not know what that would look like. I still had 90 days of training at Brownwood and Fort Stewart before the big bird took us to the desert. The pressure lifted somewhat because the separation was over now, and I could let my new reality sink in. I would have to do what I did in Basic: get through the day and wait for the freedom bird home.

The buses pulled up once again to Brownwood, Texas, and we dreaded being stacked back up in the cramped quarters until word came down that we were assigned to new buildings. We unloaded quickly and dragged our gear to the new portable buildings. I managed to claim a bottom bunk by my friend SPC Byrd, which was a major victory since I managed to surround myself with people that were considerate, easygoing, and hygienic. The sad fact is that you can be next to any number of nightmares in close quarters: soldiers with chips on their shoulders, stinking, loud, or even thieves. Yes, that did happen a few times. I kept my duffels and footlockers locked even when I went to the showers or outside to smoke. It's hard to trust those around you with your life when you can't trust them not to pocket an iPod.

I managed to link up with a solid group who would look out for each other. The building was brand new with clean showers and bathrooms or "latrines" in Army jargon, with about 50 Soldiers per building, and the females having their own. They had to bunk up with females from other companies since there were not anywhere near as many females as males. They were less than pleased with this.

Typically, when we hit the ground at a new location, our higher command scrambled with a million different things and we got batted around. The nonsense factor skyrocketed. One of my all-time favorite NCOs, SFC Lann, told me that there was some great training lined up, but they managed to schedule it so it was not as much of a beating or mad dash as it was previously. Every soldier would have to complete certified driver's training on multiple vehicles day and night, a combat lifesavers certification course, pass a PT test, combatives, a full spectrum medical evaluation, and weapons qualification on the M2 .50, 240 Bravo, and M4, several road marches, and miscellaneous PowerPoint classes and educational courses.

The days started at 445 in the morning, with a workout (PT), which alternated between run and strength training days. We usually cleaned the barracks, and then headed off to chow. Afterwards, we had about 45 minutes to get to our class locations to start the day's training. We were divided into groups for the various training events, meaning that one group was doing the medical training while another was driving, and so forth. SPC Byrd and my buddy Tom were in the same group and started with driver's training. We drove about every vehicle we could get our hands on as well as learned some basic maintenance for each vehicle. This involved day and night training so we would learn to drive with night vision and no lights, which we had to do on several occasions in Iraq. We had about an hour for lunch depending on the training and the fact we had to walk clear across the small post for the chow hall and even further for the barrack's latrine. After lunch roll call, we were back at it until final formation, which was around 1900 hours. If you had night training, you would report back in when the light was completely gone. Lights were out at 11 pm.

Bravo Company had an outstanding former active duty infantry NCO, SSG Grayson, as well as other NCO Master Drivers who taught the driver's training course. I am not an expert on the full active duty role of a Master Driver, but I know they have completed the 80 hour training online or in a classroom and qualified on a certain group of vehicles for a certain number of supervised driving hours. I completed the coursework and, strangely, was awarded the Master Driver badge at the end of my deployment. It looks like a marksmanship badge with a wheel in the center, and has different tabs, which hang off the bottom. Mine was designated "Class W" for wheeled vehicle. The tab can also designate "mechanic". I have driven very long distances in every wheeled vehicle I can think of in the Army inventory, with the exception of the Hemmitt, which is a massive recovery or heavy load vehicle.

SSG Grayson was funny, but also trained the living hell out of you. He never did anything half-assed. We took an old Humvee out to some really rocky steep areas and we went nuts. He would tell you to "speed the hell up," and drive through some serious terrain just to build your confidence. We would boulder on the thing and get to some pretty nerve-racking speeds, and drive up some *very* steep surfaces. You left the training knowing full damn well what the vehicle could and could not do. Tom, Byrd, and myself were the first on the block for night driving, and we were following chem lights (glow sticks) with noise and light restrictions. The night vision device is only on one eye, so there are some depth perception issues, but

SSG Grayson would make us drive pretty quickly while being aware of our surroundings. During one night, we had to chase another vehicle just to get used to the speed and build trust in our equipment. At daytime while others were driving, he had us doing the online training and keeping the certificates to put into our promotion folders.

After driver's training came the Combat Lifesavers certification course, which lasted one week. Primarily this class was conducted by civilian contractors who were former active duty soldiers, including some guy who was supposedly Ranger/Special Forces who was very knowledgeable and arrogant as the day is long. The purpose of the Combat Lifesaver course was to make every soldier capable of providing emergency medical care for the most common life threatening injuries: wounds from gunshots and IED explosions.

We had large workbooks and lots of practice in any number of things such as the use of the Combat Action Tourniquet (CAT) and Israeli Bandage, which was a heavy duty bandage with tightening capacity carried in the Improved First Aid Kit (IFAK). We were also trained on the use of QuikClot, which stopped bleeding by creating an artificial clot. I have heard that this was considered a substandard or ineffective product by emergency doctors and medics. I will have to trust them on that one because it is well outside my expertise.

We constantly trained on giving one another IV saline sticks. Studies found that wounded soldiers who got IV drips had a better chance of surviving. I was fairly good with this, but my veins did not want to cooperate, so I ended up getting stuck several times.

We also all became CPR certified. One of the most important things is triage, where you have to decide what injury requires attention first for best chance of survival. We also learned how to stabilize breaks and head/neck injuries. One of the most interesting events was a course in which we had to use everyday items to stop bleeding, or to create litters.

We also had to learn all the ways to carry an injured soldier. The Army had learned a harsh lesson in Iraq and Afghanistan: no one receives medical care until the battle is over. Too many soldiers were killed trying to save someone while the fight was going on. Snipers learned to wound a single soldier, not kill, so that they could shoot those who tried to save him.

The last day of the course put all the lessons together in a stressful combat-simulated situation to reinforce the skills. Overall, it was exceptional training that I could still perform to this day.

Next in good old Camp Bowie was the Pre-Deployment Health Assessment to see if there were any physical or psychiatric reasons for a soldier not to be deployed. This included any number of evaluations for hearing, injuries or recent broken bones, PTSD or depression, and dental, among many other things. This was a real wake up call for me. I was healthy and had no problems with anything that would keep me from deploying, except for some wisdom teeth they damn near pulled out before I even sat down. I had a friend from my original unit, SPC Turner, who found out he had stomach cancer. He was only five to six years older than me and he didn't even smoke. Another guy was very loud about the fact he was diagnosed with the HIV virus and was being pulled off the deployment. He actually seemed happy about that.

One of the most upsetting things to me personally was when I went out back for a smoke after a particularly boring PowerPoint session to see an old-school NCO of mine from the other company basically crying. This was surprising because he was a tough individual; I had to check up on him. Turns out his wife had lung cancer and was currently hospitalized. He had applied for a hardship exception to the deployment so he could be with his wife. Apparently, this was not a priority, and taking way too long to be approved. To the point he was about to go AWOL because he was scared she would die without him there. I made it a point to check in with him when I could and encouraged him to speak with the Chaplin to see if he could help. I heard he just left his cell number with his 1st Sergeant and left.

Next were the firing ranges without end. LT Ortega assigned SGT Dickinson, a solid female NCO who had just come off of Operation Jump Start where the Guard helped on the Mexican Border, to be the ammo noncommissioned officer in charge (NCOIC). My friend Tom, SPC Bess, and yours truly were also assigned to the detail. Let me tell you, these were some damn long days. We awoke early as hell, around 0400, to get the Light Medium Tactical Vehicle (LMTV) to the ammo point, which was a concrete storage area for the ammunition, and load it up. Often times, we had to load a majority of it by hand which was a minimum of 25 pound boxes, which had to be lifted above shoulder height to the back of the LMTV, and then drive it all to the range.

At the range, we set up some cover from the sun using old web camouflage, and pulled out thousands of rounds of ammunition in preset belt lengths for the 240 Bravo, which is a belt-fed fully automatic machine gun. We brought a cooler and camping chair and really had a good time shooting the breeze. But they were very long days in Texas heat that was always in the 90s. We would also be pulled to be range safety officers in addition to our regular duties. We were there until the night fire shooters were done, then packed up and were back at the barracks by 2300 if we were lucky. Then it started all over again. This lasted the better part of two weeks. My buddy Tom blew out his shoulder and was eventually pulled off the deployment.

...

We had reached the end of our time at Camp Bowie and we got permission from the first sergeant to take passes off the post with our spouses. Amanda picked me up after trying to figure out the back roads to Camp Bowie, and we headed to the town where we had a hotel room waiting. We managed a wonderful evening with dinner and shopping. I was dropped off too quickly the next day. It meant the world to see her and really helped me refocus. As we prepared to leave for Fort Stewart, our leadership had already left and we had some down time. As long as we signed out with CQ, we were free to come and go as we liked. I got to see a movie and go to dinner with SPC Byrd, and read some of his spy-themed fiction. He is a very talented writer. My buddy Tom lived in the area so he showed us around, and I also got to hang out with my friend SPC Stone.

Group punishment will always be at the top of irritating things in the military. As with all things, they started cancelling passes because a soldier from the artillery unit got arrested. They recalled everyone back to the post. Our passes for the evening and next day were cancelled because of this, except of course for the actual company where the soldier belonged. To me, it's as simple as bringing the hammer down on the person who can't control themselves. We are asked to take on responsibility that most people could never imagine, yet command always starts getting paternalistic and punishing the group for one knucklehead's decisions.

You can cut the hypocrisy with a knife. If some captain or lieutenant is sleeping with an enlisted soldier or gets arrested for driving while intoxicated, which I assure you happened, you won't see them calling all the officers back and locking them down.

Despite the nonsense, we all knew this would be the last of the downtime and we would hit the ground running once we got to Fort Stewart. As the buses pulled away from Brownwood, I listened to Helmet and Audioslave, knowing this would be the last time I would see Texas for a long time. Somehow, this time I was more prepared. The Army had become my everyday reality.

Chapter 6

Fort Stewart & Convoy Basics

We landed at Hunter Army Airfield—the gateway for so many headed overseas—and drove through some really gorgeous countryside on the way to Fort Stewart, Georgia. We arrived at our new barracks at the home of the 3rd Infantry Division. There, SFC Ruiz was promoted to first sergeant (E8). Considering the weight he carried, the promotion was a long time coming.

After dropping our gear on our bunks, we went to a briefing conducted by our company commander, Major Yost. During the briefing I spoke with now-First Sergeant Ruiz. He was having a hard time; the stress of managing the company through this period was taking its toll. He never spoke ill of the CO—he had more character than that—but you could tell he was carrying way more than his fair share of the load. He wasn't sleeping well and looked like he aged ten years in the last ten months. Maybe it was because the other soldiers did not know him as well as I did, but I had and still have a great deal of respect for him, while most others in the unit did not care much for him. They did not know how many times he went to bat for the enlisted soldiers against the brass, usually making his own life more difficult in the process. Unlike most, if not all, of the other senior enlisted and officers, he slept in the troops areas and spent as much time as possible on the ground overseeing training. He was the guy who fixed the laundry and food situation. He also pushed to get his people promoted and gave us slack when we needed it.

Our deployment equipment hit pretty quickly. The new interceptor body armor was put on over the head and secured around the sides with a hook and loop fastener. It was more comfortable and shifted the weight from the back, the hips, and shoulders. I was a SAW gunner, and had the full sized crew served version, which weighed about 22 pounds, not including the 1200 rounds of ammunition I carried. I was issued Para Barrels, which were much shorter and only extended a few inches past the main body of the weapon, as well as a collapsible stock which was slightly lighter, which made the weapon much easier to drag around.

Altogether, if you packed all your gear as tightly as possible, you had two duffels of just equipment with four uniforms and one extra pair of boots. Since we were only allowed a laptop case as a carry on, you had zero room for anything else that made life more livable. Honestly, they issue most of what you will need, but if you are headed out to Germany, Afghanistan, or just in a unit that spends a lot of time in the field, here are a few really useful items.

Must Have Deployment Equipment

*1. **iPod**. This one is a no brainer; but these days you can fit a full television series of your favorite shows, music, movies, and (let us be honest) porn on an iPod that only weighs a few ounces. I also recommend getting portable batteries for the iPod as well.*

*2. **The best boots you can buy.** I bought Phenix Gear Fast Assault Series boots, which required no break-in time and were authorized for wear based on our regulations. BE ADVISED, some are NOT authorized for wear. For example, if you have boots with a side zipper, they are not authorized. I also heard that the Nike Special Field Boot (SFB) was also perfect for what we do. You want them lightweight, durable, and most of all: comfortable. You cannot spend enough money on boots and socks.*

*3. **Multitool**. I carried the Gerber Suspension series and used it every single day of the deployment, and still keep it in my firing range bag to correct weapon malfunctions. Get the lightest and best one you can. Buy name brand.*

*4. **Flashlight**. I carried a powerful flashlight at all times and probably used it every day as well. I carried a mini maglight because the new-fangled LED supernova types were not around when I was deploying.*

*5. **Knife**. I carried the Gerber Paraframe because it was durable, lightweight, and I could open it with one hand. There are hundreds of name* *brands that would work just fine. If I could buy one for a deployment today, I would purchase the Black 9 Line Emergen-C knife because it has a seatbelt cutter and window breaker.*

*6. **Weatherproof Journal**. You should have a journal. Period. Writing down your thoughts is an excellent way to get perspective and process stress. Write every day and you will be way better off. You should also have a weatherproof notepad and good pen.*

*7. **Lightweight Laptop**. I had some type of IBM laptop that is now so outdated, it's ridiculous. Don't cheap out. I think the MacBook is worth the cost and you will want a DVD drive. Most have cameras and decent memory/speed. Just have a laptop and a weatherproof case.*

I was tapped by LT Ortega to be the ammo NCOIC for an M4 range to zero our newly-issued optics. Most soldiers had an M4 with an Aimpoint scope, which is a "two eye" close quarter optic that is tough and dependable with a single red dot in the center. For most situations, it is the best choice. Many were also issued ACOGs with are "one eye" scopes with usually three time or six time magnification that used ambient light to light the reticle (crosshairs). I carried the SAW which used an ELCAN scope, which was very durable and accurate and that also had some magnification.

It was a long couple of days at the range, but I got to hang out with some friends like SPC Kill and SPC Bess, who were very good natured and always keeping me laughing. Again, that element of smoke therapy, where we shoot the breeze and smoke way more cigarettes than humans should, was very helpful. That being said, I was getting over being sick from being rained on during the last week or so of training, and Amanda called and was feeling very lonely and stressed out. After two very long days we completed night fire and packed up at the end of the second day. As we were standing around waiting for the last vehicle to close up shop, LT Ortega took SPC Kill and I aside to let us know something important.

"I got out of a meeting this morning, and thought guys should know something since it is probably already been put out back at Post. I have always tried to be honest with you guys and let you know what's going on. As of this week, Iraq base security has been handed over to a contractor who used Ugandan soldiers to protect the bases. That was our mission, which means that this frees us up to shift over to a different mission. As of next week, we start training to be a convoy escort company. Not only that, but we will separate from the rest of the battalion and be sent to Joint Base Adder/Talil with the artillery battalion. To be real with you guys, this is a pretty dangerous mission we are taking on right now. Most of the casualties, which are the highest they have been in the war to this point, are during convoys. I thought you should know so you can get your heads on straight."

I was in a little bit of shock. I had it in my head that I was going to be working base security, which while dangerous, is far and away a different story than running convoys and patrols all over Iraq.

Improvised Explosive Devices (IED)

My chances of death or injury were significantly higher since IEDs were the main killer in Iraq. Most direct contact with the enemy never goes their way with our equipment, support, and training. To even the odds, they set hundreds of Improvised Explosive Devices (IEDs), which can include almost anything all along the major roadways in both Iraq and Afghanistan. Recently, they were getting even more dangerous with Explosively Formed Projectiles (EFPs) which basically were soft metals such as copper shaped into a cone with a high heat explosive placed behind it. The explosion super heats the metal and sends it flying one direction and cuts right through any armor we had. They also had Russian RKGs—grenade versions of this technology, which are thrown and parachute over the target, firing its smaller EFP into the vehicle.

An IED is a term that covers a wide range of anti-vehicle and anti-infantry explosive devices.

1. *An explosion is common to all IEDs. This can be the cause of all the damage using old artillery rounds or other explosive types where the explosion itself is the danger, or is just the carrier or force behind projectiles such as nails, ball bearings, or a copper plate.*

2. *IEDs are almost always hidden in some fairly clever places. There are always dead animals and trash on the side of the roads in Iraq and many times they hide the IED in plain sight among the garbage. They can also mount them underneath overpasses to hit our gunners as we drive under bridges. Or they simply bury them in a pothole or alongside the road, which can be very hard to detect.*

*3. **They are triggered.** We are always playing Spy vs. Spy. They come up with a new way to trigger the IEDs and we find way to diffuse or go around the trigger.*

*a. **Timer:** The most common was the timer, which was primed to explode at a certain time no matter what. This is hard to get around but they can't control if the intended target is nearby.*

*b. **Cell Phone:** Another was the cell phone detonator where they would call a number which set off the bomb when we were in range. We found ways to jam this trigger but we had to constantly evolve our technology to keep up.*

*c. **Motion Detector:** Exactly what it sounds like; it would detonate when the sensor detected movement.*

*d. **Heat sensor:** When the sensor detected a certain level of heat, above that which a normal vehicle produces, it explodes.*

*e. **Triggerman:** Finally there was the triggerman. Literally a person had a physical detonator cord strung out from the bomb and personally hit the button. This is hard to get around but we knew the signs and if they did get us, there was a good chance they would also be killed in the process when we identified them.*

Things started changing very quickly the next week. We now had 60 days to recertify from being force protection to a convoy force. We had NCOs from 1st Army to guide and grade our training, which was a high pressure situation. Pretty much all the training we received to this point did not count and we would need to recertify using their criteria. Effective immediately, the three Platoons would be broken into four Convoy Escort Teams (CETs). Lieutenant Ortega had command of two CETs: 1-6 and 2-6. LT Spears, a young former public affairs officer, would command CETs 3-6 and 4-6.

I was called by PFC Taft, who was our TOC (Company Headquarters) admin guy and told to wear my Army Combat Uniform or (ACUs) for a 1900 formation. When we showed up, several of the other specialists were in ACUs while the majority of the Company were in PTs. Specialists Wallander, Kill, Stone, Ming, and myself were lined up and promoted to corporal (CPL). I agree with the soldiers that were selected even though there were several others that would have made excellent NCOs as well. I was later promoted to sergeant and the rank was backdated somewhat. The purpose being that we simply did not have enough NCOs to fill the positions needed to run a convoy company.

...

If this were a movie, which I assure you is very unlikely; you would have to identify the main characters. Each CET would be commanded by either a lieutenant or staff sergeant as the convoy commander. An NCO would act as second in command with the title of assistant convoy commander (ACC). They assigned me to CET 2-6 under the command of SSG Lobo and SSG Sierra.

We were further divided into gun truck crews which consisted of: a driver, a gunner, and a vehicle commander. The CET medic rides with the convoy commander. The assistant convoy commander never rides in the same vehicle as the convoy commander, so if one were killed, there would still be a chain of command. We also used call signs which were pretty random in nature. Some of us used Muppets while others did their own thing. The best way to introduce my CET is by position, which will give you a frame of reference for events that occurred. The crews changed several times during the course of the deployment, but this is a basic overview.

Our scout truck was commanded by my prior service friend, CPL Wallander; call sign "Bulldog." As mentioned previously, he looked like SGT Slaughter and had a quick temper. He had served in Iraq before and knew the lay of the land pretty well. Early in the tour, his driver was a female named SPC Adriano. His turret gunner was a quiet guy named SPC Fenton.

Our second scout group ran in an Armored Security Vehicle (ASV), which had and enclosed 50 cal and Mark19 turret as well as "V" hull to deflect explosions. This was an all-female crew led by SGT Dickenson, callsign: "Slick." Her driver, SPC Bess, callsign "Rooster" had a great attitude. Her turret gunner, SPC Rhoades callsign "PopTart", loved martial arts films. My buddy Tom was originally the gunner before being pulled off the deployment due to the shoulder injury. We did not know this until much later, but they were the first all-female gun truck crew in the Army's history and had a nice little article written about them.

The pace truck was run by several NCOs but eventually fell to SPC Cooper, a mental health specialist who eventually went on to become a drill sergeant. Cooper's call sign was simply "Coop." His driver was SPC Keen, whose family had immigrated to America from Nigeria and she had a thick accent. She was also known to get very tired and erratic while driving. He had several gunners, but the standout gunner was SPC Rojo, callsign "Redman" who was a damn funny Egyptian/Hispanic medical equipment technician.

My commo/maneuver truck stayed in the center of the formation. My own call sign was "Gonzo," both to fit the Muppet theme as well as to honor Hunter S. Thompson, who I always enjoyed. My first driver was a mechanic named SPC Mathews from Boston, callsign "Boston" due to his cartoonish accent. He had a lot of problems in the past with substance abuse and would rarely listen to anyone. Typical young guy who felt he knew everything and wouldn't take shit off of anyone. He butted heads with me, the master sergeant from the motor pool, and the commander. Eventually he was parked in the motor pool and given a few photography assignments because I did not feel I could trust him to do his job outside the wire.

My next driver was a guy named SPC Baldwin, callsign "Charlie Brown" because of the size of his head; he was never without a cigarette or something to eat. He tried to scam out of the deployment in a number of ways, but once he knew he was going, he was the best damn soldier you could have with you. My gunner was a prior service Marine with a deployment to Iraq. SPC Roberts was a pure weapons expert as well as funny guy; he was also my roommate when we eventually moved to container housing. He managed to get a girl he later married knocked up when we were overseas, costing us a driver. This we all found endlessly funny.

The command vehicle was the "party bus" and held our fearless leaders. At first, SSG Lobo was the convoy commander. I used to say he was "just a pile of Mexican mustache and hate." He was a damn old school tanker from the original Gulf War who bragged he had been promoted and lost his rank twice, which I fully believe after seeing him talk with officers. He was a surly guy who truly was one of the few people who did not give a damn about subtlety. He had some health complications about halfway through the deployment and SSG Sierra took over. SSG Sierra went by the call sign "cookie monster" or simply "cookie." He was one of those ridiculously good-looking Puerto Rican guys who the females just loved. He was a solid leader and NCO and ours was by far the best CET because of this guy alone. His gunner was a young African American guy named SPC Sky, callsign "Skywalker." Sky was funny as hell.

Finally, our tail gunner truck was run by SGT Shoe, an older biomedical technician who was a prior service Navy Seabee; call sign "Shoe." He was about 6'3" and 240 lbs., and spoke like Foghorn Leghorn, country as hell and could not have been a nicer guy. He had various drivers, but the one that sticks out was a prior tour guy named SPC King who probably had some PTSD and could lose his temper very quickly. We also called him the "Porn Merchant" because he carried several external hard drives of porn and could hook up anyone on any device. The gunner was a tall guy and looked like Snoop Dog, SPC Marcus, and he was funny as hell and damn good with a .50. His call sign was "Primetime."

Our entire company, among many others, was sent out to perform our mounted (vehicle) gunnery qualifications. Credit where it is due, Fort Stewart and 1st Army had some top-notch gunnery NCOs and I learned quite a bit. Each gun crew had to qualify live fire in a moving vehicle against pop up targets designated by the training NCO. I, along with my gunner, were both qualified on every major weapon system and we were assigned the Mark 19, which is a belt fed grenade launcher. We were having major problems with the T & E bar, which allows the weapon to elevate and traverse, on the assigned weapon. My gunner was a badass and just "free-gunned" the monster, meaning he just manually elevated and traversed the weapon (lift and fire), which was 72 pounds without ammo. All he had to balance and distribute the weight was a crappy bipod mount on the canvas Humvee.

We were set up in a massive tent about the size of an average gymnasium, sleeping on cots about 2-3 feet apart without shower facilities. It rained constantly and it was hot as hell. Then there was a very unceremonious change in command. I had returned from yet another rotation as ammo NCO to find the hive all stirred up. Apparently Major York returned to find his gear removed from the area and there was a hasty formation in my absence where our new commander was introduced to us. Captain Jason Bellevue assumed command of Charlie Convoy Company. I don't really know what happened with Major York, I barely knew the guy. Word was that he pissed off our battalion commander, who relieved him in place.

Captain Bellevue was an Arlington police officer and an infantry officer, callsign: "Five-O." He served as a corpsman (medic for Marines) in the Navy before coming over to the Army side of the house. He told us many stories, which seemed like quite tall tales, leading to his affectionate nickname "Jason Bourne" from the series of action novels and movies. Initially, he was very hesitant to take over a medical company, which was now magically a convoy security unit. During gunnery he realized Charlie had the highest gunnery scores of the battalion and actually worked pretty well as a unit, mostly thanks to our NCOs. He and I spoke at length several times. He is very funny, genuinely tough, and had a spine. We were better off as a company headed into combat with him than Major York. He very much became Chuck Norris to the enlisted guys, with a series of jokes. For example:

1. They can never name a bridge after Captain Bourne, because no one crosses Captain Bourne.
2. A rattlesnake once bit Captain Bourne, and after three painful days, the snake finally died.
3. Captain Bourne can start a fire by rubbing two Hajis together.
4. You can't put Captain Bourne's location in your Dagger (GPS) because he is always right behind you.
5. Captain Bourne once threw a grenade which killed 50 Hajis... before it exploded.

We went through these firing orders again and again. I think these days are so vivid in my memory because of the pace of the training. I was an NCO and one NCO had to be with the ammo depot at all times, issuing and tracking ammo. I almost got into a fistfight with a jackass from another company who could not issue me a correct ammo count, so I refused to assume responsibility until he unscrewed himself. If something was wrong or went missing, it would not be during my watch. These were usually six hour shifts, then I would be shifted to gate guard of the range before heading back to work on our notoriously unreliable Humvees or to clean the weapon system. I never really slept more than four to five hours and I was working as a sergeant with corporal stripes, meaning I was not making one nickel more than a specialist for working a hell of a lot harder. It really made me rethink accepting the direct commission, but I figured this was only a year and change left to go, where if I joined as an officer they would have me for at least eight more.

Following the gunnery tables, we had a week or so of relatively easy training and sleeping in air conditioning before the next field exercise. The next round was reactive fire and urban tactical training. During one exercise, I was assigned as a SAW gunner on a vehicle and got to put fire on OPFOR (soldiers pretending to be bad guys) with blanks and MILES gear. We reacted so quickly they did not have an opportunity to mount a full attack. Apparently they said they pretty much "killed" everyone on the prior group and we performed well.

We set up in a final convoy training exercise, which was quite good. We really had to learn how to map out our routes and protect our assets in a very long mission, which stretched from day to night. We learned to shut down threats and be aware of the enemy tactics and techniques that had proven so deadly for our forces in Iraq. Gunners had to be aware of overpasses and stay as low in the turret as possible, as most of our gunners were standing in the turret when they were killed. Standing gunners present a better target, or were more exposed to a blast. The training cadre really emphasized the use of equipment such as flame retardant uniforms, gloves, and safety glasses to reduce common injuries from IED blasts and shrapnel. At this point in the training, we were planning, executing, and evaluating our own performance, and things started to come together pretty well.

We were reaching the end of our time at Fort Stewart and I am really only able to describe a fraction of the training we conducted and how tiring it can all be. Most Americans will never know the level of work that the average Joe puts into the military. I remember a couple of pretty tough road marches as well as some very easy ones. One in particular was brutal because I was carrying the SAW in soft sand with all my gear on. Someone passed out and the first sergeant and I had to render aid, and apparently they had to be evacuated out. One road march we wore our rucks, and at the end I watched an NCO put down his light-as-a-feather ruck after bragging about the time he made. He got real ass hurt when I lifted his ruck with two fingers and called him a pussy; especially when LT Spears, who was a 110-pound female, had a ruck heavier than most of us. My favorite bit was that I traded in my M249 SAW for an M4 rifle and it was like my birthday and Christmas all at once. A big thank you to my buddy Steve for making that exchange happen; it's good to know the supply guys.

...

We had finally been certified to deploy and now we had a three day pass to go home. I bought a plane ticket on the first flight out, and caught a ride with my former squad leader and his wife to the airport. I was told there may be delay or that a flight was to be overbooked. I shamelessly approached the airline lady and told her I only had 72 hours home and really could not spend it at the airport. I was put on the flight and then I was upgraded to first class on the next flight to Dallas Fort Worth, where my beautiful fiancé was waiting along with my friends Rick and Cindy. Amanda looked so different. Her hair was much longer and a different color; and she wore a gorgeous dress for me. We drove north as fast as possible to get home.

I remember standing in my bedroom staring at my worn-out boots and faded uniform piled in the corner. I put on jeans and a t-shirt. It was like stepping onto Mars. This was not the fast-paced life I was used to; I could sleep and eat whatever and whenever I wanted. I was not responsible for anyone but myself. My wife was cooking in the other room and my Labradors were hanging out on the bed. I ate a meal with my family and my brother's wife's family. We walked around a lake by my house with the dogs and talked. I was very thin at this point, weighing in at about 175 pounds at 5'11". I always looked a little heavier even though I did well on PT tests in my career; I just have that body style.

The good days bleed out fast, and on the third day, the pressure was back on my shoulders. I was leaving again soon and it would be a while before I saw Texas again. I bought my wife some earrings and had a family dinner at a Thai food place where they gave me some excellent gifts. Morning came and we had breakfast and it was damn hard to say goodbye to my dogs. My wife and I drove to Dallas and had to turn around after about 30 minutes because we forgot her phone. I was grateful for the extra time. We held hands and listened to NPR and podcasts and arrived with time to spare at DFW airport. I was not going to make the same mistake as last time. We stayed together holding each other or just standing until the moment I had to get back on the plane. As I boarded, I watched her leave and tried to keep my voice from breaking.

I met up with CPL Ming who told me he spent money drinking and partying since he did not have a family. *Party like it's your last time, it just might be.*

We arrived after going through Atlanta to Savanna, and then to Fort Stewart. It was game time.

Chapter 7

Kuwait

We cleared out the barracks at Fort Stewart and stood by our duffel bags for several hours. The guys ordered a bunch of pizzas and I shot the breeze with SPC Byrd, read my *Odd Thomas* book, or simply listened to my iPod and smoked. This is a quintessential part of the Army: waiting for something to happen.

Finally we loaded our gear onto a truck then boarded the buses headed to Hunter Air Field. I will never forget that wherever the bus went, people knew what it meant. People stopped and saluted, waved, or got out of the way. It really meant something to me; that respect from the other soldiers. When we got there we had to be weighed and sorted into groups. I had some time to call my fiancé and brother, since once I was on the plane the phone was useless until I got back home. There were older civilian volunteers who were amazing, providing food and support to thousands before us and thousands that were to come. These people demonstrated patriotism and honor. I have a profound sense of gratitude for these people. They watch you go and welcome you home.

We boarded our planes and then came a series of bizarre movements. When we finally boarded, I was stopped because I had my Gerber knife on my body armor and was told it would have to be stowed. I explained I also had an M4 Rifle as well, which may also be a threat. She stated it had no ammunition; I explained it was still an eight pound steel and polymer club and more dangerous than the knife if wielded properly. Of course I lost this argument, and had to find a way to stow my blade. We put our armor and weapons under the seats and settled in for a very, very long trip.

I had bought nicotine patches and passed a few out to smokers such as myself. We landed for a few short hours in Canada before a very long 12-14 hours in the air landing in Shannon, Ireland, which was beautiful. I stood outside smoking with my friend SPC Dayton, who we called "Drill" since he was a prior service drill sergeant, and marveled at how green it all looked. I wanted more than anything to be one of the other American tourists or Irish citizens landing and going on vacation or just going about their normal lives. I ordered breakfast and enjoyed coffee while reading a magazine. Already other soldiers were dropping money on stuff they would not need. Such is the nature of young people and money. Time flew by and we got back on for the next leg of the flight to Kuwait.

It was at this point I was in a window seat watching Europe pass by below me, feeling my place in the span of history. Fear was in the forefront of my mind. While I was afraid that I would not return at all, I was more afraid of being one of the casualties I saw at Fort Sam Houston. I was afraid I would lose a limb, my sight, or be burned to the point the picture on the ID card was not recognizable as the same person. These were real fears, yet despite all of that I had another concern on my mind. I was afraid my relationship with my fiancé would not survive. We were four plus months or so into the deployment, and several marriages and couples had split up, some in very ugly ways.

I struggled with writing about my thoughts on this particular subject because I am still friends with many from the deployment. It would be a lot easier to write about mortars, IEDs, and firefights than to discuss a reality of deployment: infidelity (it's not just for infidels anymore). I watched people say tearful goodbyes to their kids and wives as well as fiancés and girlfriends, only to see them fooling around less than a month later. I know there is not one soldier reading this book that does not know exactly what I am talking about. I heard several times that "what happens on deployment stays on deployment." Several guys contracted STDs, and several of the female soldiers became pregnant.

Now comes the honest part: I was very tempted. It was made clear to me that some girls were interested. It was very difficult to say no. Putting young, fit people in their sexual prime in an extreme high-stress environment and expecting there not to be fooling around is simply unrealistic. Other soldiers would tell me in detail who, what, and when of who they were sleeping with. More surprising to me was that soldiers would mess around with some girl or contractor and be shocked when they, in turn, messed around with someone else. Oh, the drama and betrayal. These same people would then be disgusted and offended when their spouses or significant others admitted they were unfaithful.

This happened in all ranks in the chain of command, all the way to the very top. It was harder to say who was not messing around than who was. I am not an angel, nor do I live in an ivory tower of judgment. I get it. At times I needed sex as much as I needed air, but I was careful to never put myself in a situation where I might break. I did not even want to give the appearance of my messing around. There was also the reality that many of the spouses back home were being unfaithful while their significant others were deployed. At least two soldiers I know returned from the deployment to wives that were gone along with all of their money from the deployment, leaving behind a mountain of debt.

...

On the flight to Kuwait, the possibilities were clear on the road before me. Acceptance is an important aspect of deployment. We were soldiers with a mission. Life and death were in the hands of the people around me, many having not reached their 21st year of life. While I don't want to sound cold hearted, the thought of killing never bothered me. I have no moral barrier to killing. I do not wish to kill, but that is the nature of war and staying alive. They will make the choice to attack me or my soldiers and we will use everything at our disposal to destroy them. Some soldiers can't wait for combat, and to me that is Hollywood in their minds. I imagine them hearing a soundtrack in their heads while they practice their heroics.

The reality of combat is fear, confusion, and survival.

We landed at night and unloaded from the plane. I am not sure what I was expecting, but Captain Bourne said a bus full of troops was a great target for a bomb and we would be driving through Kuwait on the way to the base. The NCOs on the ground loaded us onto a bus with the windows covered by curtains, supposedly so we couldn't be identified as soldiers as we were driving through Kuwait. Two Soldiers were given one magazine apiece of ammunition to protect each bus, which seemed ludicrous. SGT Pine laughed and said we could walk to base without the slightest real threat in Kuwait. I was really not expecting all this secret squirrel-type CIA blackout silliness.

We drove for about 45 minutes in the night and arrived at Camp Buehring, Kuwait. This Camp was named to honor LTC Charles Buehring who was killed in action (KIA) in Baghdad on 26 October, 2003. Dawn was breaking, and our internal clocks were all fairly jacked up. Our entire battalion filed into a massive tent and watched a welcome video and we were briefed by some self-important officer. If you have to explain why we should respect you, that ship has probably already sailed. I even saw my XO roll his eyes.

A quick word on the XO, I was planning on calling him CPT Nelson but in a recent conversation he wished to be referred to as "Nighthawk" in this book. I find this endlessly hilarious and will grant him this wish. So anytime I refer to the Company Executive Officer, it will be as CPT Nighthawk. He was a first lieutenant when this whole shebang kicked off but was promoted in the first few months of the deployment. He is a talented guitarist and genuinely gave a damn about his soldiers. He did not feel he had to play a role or snarl to be respected; he could read the nonsense in the Army pretty well and did not dance to the fiddle. I smoked many cigarettes and played many songs with this guy and he really kept a lot of weirdness from being dropped on us. More importantly, he stuck up for the guys in the field against the whims of higher command. Again, a real leader does not kick his people under the bus to make his own life easier.

By the time the dog and pony show had ended, it was daylight outside. All around the camp were large dunes of shifting sand, and the roads were lined with concrete blast walls painted with unit emblems. Tents and a few hard structures dotted the landscape. It looked like we invaded Tattooine from Star Wars, kept a look out for Jawas. We walked to a location where our gear was unloaded and we were assigned tents based on our CETs and platoons. I dropped my gear next to my crew and we left a gear guard as we headed to the chow hall to eat until our next formation.

I walked with SPC Byrd down to the chow hall where hundreds of British soldiers were lined up. I was fascinated by them and we traded weapons for inspection. One had an Enfield SA80, which was a bad ass 5.56 caliber "bullpup" rifle, meaning that the trigger was near the front while the barrel, chamber, and magazine well were in the back. Basically the design was just as accurate, but did not stick out ahead of the soldier holding it as far. I also checked out their version of the SAW (squad machine gun) which was pretty damn similar to ours, probably even the same manufacturer. Their rank structure was similar, but corporals and sergeants commanded more soldiers overall. They asked whether or not I had been drafted! It was interesting that was the common belief. They loved the fact I was from Texas, along with all the stereotypical beliefs about Texas. I had them convinced I owned several ranches which produced horsemeat, which was a delicacy.

They were warriors; every one of them, and we were glad to have them with us.

After chow and a shower, we had a formation explaining we would probably be in Kuwait for about two weeks before flying into Adder/Talil; a joint military base by Nasiriyah in Iraq which was one of the largest cities. The Army called the base Adder and the Air Force called it Talil; we called it both but more often it was Talil. We had some training lined up and the unit we were replacing had sent down a team of convoy NCOs to help the transition.

The first day at Buerhing was fairly tame. We were issued our ammunition and some of us had random tasks assigned. Otherwise we could PT and get acclimated to the heat. It was hot as hell in Kuwait, far worse than Iraq in my opinion. Sand gets in absolutely everything almost immediately. I was surprised how established Buehring was: full performance stage, theater, several call centers, computer labs, several chow halls, a PX the size of a Wal-Mart with a "haji market," where Americans could buy silly crap.

The first day or so was death by PowerPoint, followed by some high-speed live fire convoy lanes, which took us to many mock villages and combat situations. We slept on the hard floor of the classroom then went back to convoy the next day. Apparently a couple of soldiers managed to bump uglies in a packed room without anyone noticing; hats off, I guess. The live fire was really fun, and the second day of this training we drove and fired on targets with our own weapon systems, and we also worked on some navigation techniques. By the end of the second week, we had established pretty solid Standard Operating Procedures (SOPs).

The final days in Kuwait were spent with my buddy CPL Wallander in a Blue Force Tracker Class. Without getting specific, it is basically a computer/GPS system mounted in military vehicles and was vital to identifying dangers and communicating with your command and other friendly forces. During that time, we were able to eat fast food and get some amazing Green Beans coffee at lunch. It was as easy as Army life ever really gets.

Back at Camp Buehring we started getting geared up and ready to leave when given the final orders. Large scale troop movements are kept secret until the last minute in order to keep terrorists from planning an attack. Operational Security or OPSEC is keeping vital information from our enemies by not spreading information that people don't need to know. I once gave a briefing on OPSEC where I used MySpace to figure out information on individual soldiers that were on the roster, such as where they lived, what their families looked like, and where they went to school. OPSEC is simple things like burning or shredding addresses and phone numbers, and not discussing your unit with civilians, even if they are friends.

We did not know when exactly we would be leaving, just to be prepared. I had Thanksgiving by myself in a chow hall in Kuwait while reading a book, and early the next morning we were on buses to the airfield bound for Talil, Iraq. I remember smoking a cigarette and talking with SFC Rocha and LT Ortega, talking about how damn glad we were to be done with all the train up and rushing around and to just start our damn mission already. I felt like a live wire. I was young, fit, well trained and well-armed. We were all nervous and scared every time we left the wire; anyone who says otherwise is probably lying. We all found ways to set that aside and do our jobs. I had secret clearance and let me tell you, an enemy intelligence briefing is one of the most sobering experiences you can have in a lifetime. There are people out there trying their best to kill you, and sometimes you can't do a damn thing about it.

Chapter 8

Iraq

We landed in Talil, Iraq and were briefed by NCOs regarding the post and then dragged our gear to the tents we were assigned. The tents were actually not bad. They had working air conditioning, and there were only 11 of us per tent. We dropped gear then walked to the chow hall to grab something to eat before the next formation. I was shocked. The chow hall was a hardened concrete building surrounded by blast walls with a full kitchen, flat screen TVs, and a buffet-style set up, with three meals a day with some night service as well. You could get something grilled or just grab cereal or a sandwich. It was pretty easy for Fobbits (soldiers who never went outside the wire), guys who never sweated in heavy body armor on missions, to fatten up nicely. Talil had a large Post Exchange Shopping center, internet cafes, a Green Beans Coffee Company, and the Talil Market commonly referred to as the "Haji Mart" where shrewd locals pimped cheap crap to dumb soldiers, myself included. Honestly, if I had to choose where to be posted in Iraq, this would be it. With a few notable exceptions where I was intimately involved, we were rarely mortared and it was nowhere near as densely packed with soldiers like the other Posts we visited.

You have probably heard some terminology in some recent shows and movies, but here are a few common ones to Iraq.

1. *Fobbit: Most posts were commonly referred to as Forward Operating Bases or (FOBs). The term Fobbit came from FOB + Hobbits (who never leave the Shire). A Fobbit never goes outside the wire and is currently not in a combat position. A majority of the military on the FOB are there in a support role. This can lead to bitterness or lack of insight regarding combat related matters because Fobbits, don't know first hand what they are talking about, yet still make very important decisions for combat troops.*

2. *EOD: Explosive Ordinance Disposal. True damn heroes; Navy or Army Engineers who disarm bombs.*

3. *Haji- This basically applies to Iraqi or Afghani citizens as well as anything cheap, worn out, half-assed, or outright stolen. For example: I went to the market to get some Haji DVDs and a Rolex. Or when applied to people: "We have six Hajis 50 meters at our nine o'clock." While I realize this is offensive, if you want an honest portrayal of how we spoke, this is it. I feel that massaging the truth to be more palatable robs one of an actual perspective of the regular soldier on the ground in Iraq. I, nor most soldiers, harbor the Iraqi people any particular ill will and certainly don't hate them. They are like anyone else, most of them decent people trying to get by.*

After the sprint that was training, we were all expecting to hit the ground running. Not the case; we had trainings but they were reasonably timed and things were set a reasonable pace for damn near the first time in the whole deployment. We attended a series of trainings and briefings by the 7th Sustainment Brigade, whom we fell under for the first few months. This was the first time I experienced "outgoing" where our artillery fires off "missions" and it's loud enough to shake the ground and can be heard and felt anywhere on the FOB. I thought we were being shelled, but no one else seemed worried so I carried on. We had a formation which said that because of the massive influx of troops from the Surge we would likely remain in the tents for most of the deployment. People were fairly irritated about this, but it honestly did not bother me too much. The tents had AC and were fairly nice; I was damn used to living in close quarters by this point in the deployment.

My driver, SPC Mathews, had one hell of a chip on his shoulder. We called him "Boston," and he got into an argument with SGT Shoe and was very disrespectful. SPC Byrd called him out on this and Boston lost his temper and it almost broke out into a fight. I took him outside and let him smoke and talked some sense into the kid. It's a constant cycle where the guy's mouth fires faster than his brain and he refuses to take responsibility for himself or his actions. I have had to keep myself from losing it with the kid a dozen times. Nothing works because there were no consequences. We spent the majority of our time stacked on top of one another in vehicles or training in a stressful environment that no matter how well you liked anyone, tempers and patience gave out eventually.

...

We were assigned our vehicles and began our "right seat/left seat" with the outgoing artillery battery (a "battery" is the equivalent of a company) out of Fort Sill. Right seat/left seat is where we ride along while they conduct normal operations, then we take over operations with the outgoing unit acting in a hands-off advisory role. They were really some pretty squared away soldiers and excellent instructors, but sucked at maintaining their vehicles. When we saw the vehicles, they were sporting some major mechanical issues. My ASV had a nasty hydraulic leak under the turret floor plates and was dangerously low on oil. The SINCGAR radios were only half working and one was not even hooked up to the antenna. We basically had two ASVs, one MRAP, two up-armored Humvees, and an LMTV. These vehicles were not built to operate in brutally hot and sand-polluted conditions every day all day. Credit where it was due, we had some good mechanics but they only had limited parts and supplies to fix a lot of our problems.

Stationed in Talil, every mission began with us driving to Cedar II, a small FOB about 15 minutes outside of Talil where the contractors and Third Country Nationals (TCNs) who were paid next to nothing to drive unarmored vehicles from poor countries, were parked and ready to go. We drove primarily three missions to the following bases: Logistics Base Seitz, Camp Taji, and Joint Base Balad.

**Home base: Talil/Adder** is near Nasiriyah (pronounced Nah-sir-e-yah), which is in the far southeast in Iraq and one of the largest cities. There was a Romanian section of the base called "Camp Dracula"; I am not making that up. This area is notable for being right next to the **Ziggurat of Ur,** which is a massive pyramid-like structure built in the Bronze Age about 2000 years before Christ. This was the center of a large city which was the center of a state which controlled much of Mesopotamia at the time. The Ziggurat served as a temple and administrative center and was built by King Ur-Nammu.

**Scania:** Convoy Support Center Scania was about halfway, maybe less, in a convoy's journey north. This was not a large military installation, but had several fuel points for our vehicles as well as maintenance units and contractors. This was not a large facility; it was surrounded on all sides with protected checkpoints and high blast walls. One of the few times we stayed overnight, we discovered it had a small coffee kiosk and a small Post Shopping Exchange.

**Logistics Base Sietz:** This base was about two hours south of Camp Taji and our missions there were the shortest of the three. The base itself was south of what was called the "Sunni Triangle" or, as we called it, "Sunni-ritaville" aka "Mortar-ritaville." It was shelled on a regular basis. I loved getting these missions because it usually meant that our total mission time would be less than eight hours instead of twelve or more, like when we headed to Taji or Balad. While it had all the bells and whistles of a larger post, I really did not care for it because our temporary barracks were hellish and far from everything. The bus system took forever to get anywhere. I usually caught up on my reading when staying overnight here.

**Camp Taji:** Taji was about 20 miles or so north of Baghdad and was one of the larger military bases in the country. It was the primary post for most of the Surge troops. This base had every bell and whistle, including an actual movie theater and a massive marketplace selling damn near anything you could get stateside. I was shocked when I first saw it.

**The Boneyard:** Located in Camp Taji was the boneyard of hundreds of destroyed and abandoned tanks from Saddam's Republican Guard. It was a sight to see that much armor lined up and rotting.

Joint Base Balad: aka Camp Anaconda. This was the most massive and densely-packed base in my opinion and had every amenity you could ask for. Most of the big USO shows went through here. We stayed in "chicken coops" which were like office cubicles with a cot in them. I am not exaggerating when I say we were mortared at least once every single time we were there. The most dangerous trip a convoy could make at the time was Camp Taji was to Balad. Most of the IEDs that resulted in casualties were on this stretch of the road, and this was where we had to be at the top of our game. This was also the furthest trip, even though it was only about 30 miles north of Taji. The average mission time was sometimes in excess of twelve hours from Talil to Balad.

Chapter 9

Outside the Wire

Those first missions, our nerves were blasted. We knew that the violence had dropped since the Surge began, but convoys were getting hit every day. Every day our forces were finding, disarming, or destroying many IEDs. The borders to Iraq were wide open with bombs and weapons flooding into the country daily. In Taji, one of the medevac NCOs told me about a young female second lieutenant who lost both legs on her very first mission outside of the wire on convoy. I was one of the few NCOs that had a security clearance and attended the briefings, and saw all the cute little PowerPoint explosion points and casualty reports. We saw bombs everywhere we looked, and we pushed the traffic far away from us as we were expecting the vans to roll right up to us and detonate. We were lucky to have NCOs like Lobo, Wallander, and Sierra who had been here before and could usually tell the difference between a real and imagined threat.

We learned fairly quickly that the route south of Scania was, while not safe, much less likely to result in an IED strike or direct attack. My gunner, SPC Roberts, had spliced some iPod headphones into the audio system of the ASV and we were listening to music and chain smoking cigarettes when the SINCGAR radio squawked to life.

"Big Bird, this is Coop. One of the KBR contractors pulled up next to us and is trying to flag us down!"

"Roger, Coop. Halt the Convoy"

We halted the convoy and my driver drove out of column formation to get better eyes down the length of the long line of trucks. I heard the high pitched whine of the hydraulic turret shifting from position to position to scan for enemies. There was supposed to be a radio between the lead KBR truck and one of our gun trucks, but it never really worked. Most of us figured there was a blown tire or mechanical issue, which happened at least once per mission. We lit another smoke and started our slow security movements when the radio squawked again.

"Big Bird, we had an attack on one of our vehicles. The driver said a white SUV drove up and started yelling, then fired an AK. Break. He has some cuts from the glass and holes all in the door, window and windshield. Over."

"Roger. Fuck. Shut down the traffic and push these other civilians either around off the highway or they stay where they are. Over." Then he called for me. "Gonzo, Big Bird."

"This is Gonzo, send it," I said.

"Gonzo, you get back here with me in the rear. Cookie and the Doc can see the driver and hold the center while Slick and Bulldog hold up the front. Break. All units: search around for an IED and keep an eye out for that white SUV. If you see a rifle, light 'em the fuck up."

We drove to the rear of the convoy as I got on my second radio to the "land owner." Every section in our route from one base to another was operated by a land owner, which is the major military command of that sector. I contact them to let them know we are entering/leaving their Area of Operations (AO). If anything happened in their sector, they were responsible for providing a response. They were able to provide a Quick Response Force (QRF), as well as support and medevac. We happened to be right in the middle of two such territories; one in Talil and one in a FOB called Kasul. We really did not need any assistance at this point, but we felt they should be aware. It just so happened, another convoy had just dropped their escorts in Cedar II and offered to come and lend assistance. Communication is one of the most important things in a combat zone.

We arrived in the back of the convoy and things were already ugly. Vehicles were stacked up behind the convoy. Hundreds of people, without exaggeration, were out of their vehicles, irritated, and cooking in the Iraq sun. We pulled our ASV up parallel with the Humvee and the twin .50 caliber and Mark 19 barrels added some credibility to our position if it kicked off into a firefight.

It's never good to have hundreds of angry Iraqis. It helps to see it from their position sometimes. Imagine that Iraqis occupied America and shut down the largest highway in your home town. They have not explained why and just stand there and not let you go anywhere. You can't back up because of all the traffic behind you, and if you don't have an SUV then you can't go on the soft desert sand on either side of the highway. Also imagine it is a heat wave to the tune of 105 degrees and you either don't have or can't afford air conditioning in your car. You could have an elderly person or a kid with you as well. Now tell me how patient and calm you are going to be.

There a dozen major problems with crowd control in Iraq. Top of the list includes the crowd itself. That is what makes an insurgency and guerilla tactics so successful. They do not wear uniforms and can blend into a crowd perfectly. Someone could take a shot at you then turn and walk away; you would never know who just tried to kill you. Also, if we did start receiving small arms fire from a vehicle that was backed up or from the crowd, we would be very limited in our response. Our options would be to return fire with our crew served weapons, which would mean the rounds would travel through several people and vehicles before coming to a stop; or use our rifles hoping to pick out a few shooters from a confused and scared crowd, keeping our fingers crossed we did not shoot up a bunch of kids on accident. Finally, bomb vests and vehicle-borne IEDs (VBIEDS) can cause a lot of damage, and the insurgents don't care who they kill, as long as they take out Americans. A VBIED had been used the week before outside of Taji, so we had to force the Iraqis to keep their distance.

Our vehicles were set up to stop or force traffic around the cordon (perimeter) we established. A rule of thumb was to keep vehicles and people back three hundred meters. Due to the nature of this pileup, they were actually only 100-150 meters away. This did not give us a lot of breathing room to make a decision to fire if someone started acting froggy. Big Bird had lit a cigar and was on the ground next to me, alternating between talking on the radio and helping cover the crowd, which was growing by the second. I was cooking; it was well over 100 degrees on a blacktop road and we were wearing about 40-50 pounds of gear and ammo as well as gloves and eye protection which always fogged up.

Then I noticed another problem. There was a tall balding Iraqi man who had a clean shaved face and head, which was unusual, and he seemed to be instigating the crowd. He would yell and point at us and some of the crowd started to agree that they had had enough. He would yell for a while then walk towards us a few steps to test our response, then walk back and start yelling and rabble-rousing again. Any given Sunday, soldiers have to make decisions that could end up on CNN. If we fired on this guy because we were worried he was a threat and happened to blast a civilian or kid in the process, we had to live with that. If we didn't shoot him and it ended up he had a bomb vest and killed my soldiers, we had to live with that too. I knew he was not done, and I was expecting the crowd to start throwing rocks, which is basically a national pastime of the kids over there, especially when you don't give them food or water when they are begging.

"Watch that fucker, Gonzo," SSG Lobo said.

"Roger, I got him," I said, growing concerned and eyeing him while trying to watch the rest of the crowd through the heat waves of the blacktop.

The man turned, thinking he had enough support to walk up and give us a piece of his mind. Thing is, that even with a language barrier, he knew what a rifle pointed at him meant. As he walked closer, my rifle began to raise in his direction. He did the math and understood. To be sure, he started walking closer as my rifle continued to rise until it was almost pointed dead center at his chest. Worry spread across his face.

"That fucker crosses the 50 meter mark, you fire a warning shot; he keeps coming, you drill him and I will back you up," SSG Lobo snarled as he pointed for the guy to head back to the crowd.

At this point, with my rifle almost pointed square at him, he walked back to the crowd. It was tense; he was about one step from the warning shot and a few more until he got himself a permanent souvenir. I could hear the whirring of the ASV turret and Big Bird's gunner was about to shoot him with a flare, which would have been really funny. I lit a smoke and was glad it went down the way it did. A lot of the tension we carry is not when an IED goes off or when we are actually fired upon; it's the life and death decisions and near misses. Thankfully, the Iraqi police showed up at this point and started helping with crowd control.

I was called back to the ASV because Big Bird needed me on the radio relaying information to the land owners and friendlies in the area. Apparently, one of our gunners had spotted the white SUV backed up in the traffic. When the driver realized we had spotted them, they made a break for it. The SUV drove off road into the soft sand and attempted to drive around our perimeter. Slick's ASV dove off after them and chased them down. After a short pursuit, the ASV was parked directly in front of the Chevy Suburban with both barrels leveled at them. The .50 caliber was only a breath away, ready to eviscerate the vehicle and obliterate its occupants. Bulldog's gunner also had a bead on them with the 240 Bravo, and if they moved again, it probably would have been an ugly death.

Kasul's Quick Reaction Force (QRF) pulled the men out of the SUV and pulled out several large bags, including one that obviously held large metallic objects, probably rifles. We were playing stupid games of letting the Iraqis; many corrupt as the day was hot, handle their own people. This is where every soldier can relate. This is where things always got stupid when higher command got involved. The other convoys showed up and were helping us recover our vehicle and assist with crowd control. The Iraqi police detained and searched the SUV. Word came down from the landowner and command that we were to let the Iraqis handle it from there and we were to RTB (return to base). Bullshit. These guys fired on our convoy and now the keystone cops were going to let them walk.

When we got back to Adder, Captain Bourne was pissed, but not at us. Honestly, we handled this as well as could be expected, and any day you have all your people and you did not have an international incident is a good day. Captain Bourne said we were probably within our rights to have fired on them with the threat they presented. Bare minimum; next time kick them out of their vehicle and bring it home. While I am not sure if he was kidding on that, he was correct that our instincts were dead on. Hard to say what should have happened, and people at the FOB are always ready to armchair quarterback and say what should have been done.

Hell of a day.

Chapter 10

Tales from the Sandbox

Indirect fire is a hell of a thing. This term applies to mortars and rockets that are fired at our FOBs on a regular basis, sometimes on a daily basis. They are very hard to stop because it only takes a tube or a hill and some 2x4s in order to fire off lethal rounds at Americans; then you can pack up and be gone before the Americans come looking.

Indirect fire happened very rarely at Talil. A few mortars were fired near the post, and a few times we were hammered pretty well out by our Head Quarters Building and Chapel at Talil. One time we were hit, a stray mortar also hit the Ziggurat of Ur. This pissed off the locals, and I heard the local tribes ended up killing the people who fired the mortars. Then let us know they killed them.

Some FOBs like Balad and Seitz were hit every day, causing casualties and damaging housing and equipment. They had a system called the Counter Rocket, Artillery, and Mortar (C-RAM), which picked up incoming mortars or rockets with its sensors and shot them out of the sky. You could hear them all the time in Balad when we had incoming; the sound of a mechanical turret spinning and then the overwhelming sound of paper tearing as thousands of bullets blow the incoming out of the sky before it can detonate on the ground. We were hit so many times in Balad; we all just stopped even getting out of bed to head to the bunkers.

It was January 20th, and it was my 28th birthday. We had returned from mission the day before and I had the whole day to basically waste and I was taking full advantage. We slept during the day since our missions took place at night when we had an advantage over the enemy due to our night vision. I had spent the day working out, reading, and screwing around on the internet. My brother sent me an Xbox and SPC Roberts and I had moved into our new Combat Housing units (CHUs), which consisted of tiny apartments with about 300 square feet to share between two soldiers. We bought a bunch of Haji pirated movies and were wasting the day. Roberts asked me to go to evening chow; I said I would meet him there since I had a few more things to do. When I finished up, I grabbed my rifle and stepped outside for a smoke before I walked the several blocks to the chow hall. I remember thinking about how different my next birthday would be: back home, married, working on my graduate degree. I was in a good mood. The missions pace had increased, but we had settled into a nice rhythm.

I walked into the open from the blast walls protecting the CHUs and glanced up toward the PX and DFAC where my brain had a hard time processing what I saw. Time seemed to slip into slow motion as I saw what seemed like a shooting star headed right at me. The sound was surreal, like a deck of cards being hard shuffled and amplified through a wall of speakers with almost a deafening tearing sound. I remember not even thinking I was in danger, just wondering what the hell I was seeing; time dripped like molasses. The only way I can describe it is as "time expansion" or lengthening of the time between moments. It was heading directly at me, and then seemed to shift to my right at the last moment. It hit the ground and exploded.

It was deafening for an instant, and then it sounded like I fell in a pool of water, as if my ears just turned themselves down. I realized I had hit the ground; I was in shock, it was chaos. Smoke and dust filled the air all around me and I was genuinely scared because the explosion was very close and I did not know what to do. I was expecting more incoming. I stood on a slight elevation next to low ground before the blast walls protecting the CHUs, and the rocket had struck to the five o'clock of where I was just standing, about 30-40 meters away. The whole area behind me was smoke and dust and I could not really hear or see much in that direction. Time was dripping away as my mind struggled to start working again.

I watched the soldiers in view from my forward and left scramble for cover. Seemed like a great idea. I started to run and almost tripped over an iron cord on the ground which separated the parking from living area. I started to run back to the blast walls, then ran toward a bunker to my far left, my mind racing until a thought burst into my brain which stopped me in my tracks. I had no idea who was behind me when the rocket hit. Someone could have been killed or wounded. I must have looked like a cat with a head injury, because I changed direction again and started running back. I ran and looked around and did not see any other soldiers. I could not see through the smoke at the center of the impact, but I put eyes all around and called out. At this point, I ran my ass off toward the bunker.

An arm snaked out and snatched me inside. An older soldier was grabbing at me and checking me over. A younger soldier watched and seemed amused.

"You are in shock, son! I am checking for wounds, you may not know you are hit!" yelled the soldier. "Holy shit! You were right there! I really thought that got you until you stood up!"

"I could use a smoke…" I managed. My heart was beating a thousand times a second.

The young soldier fired up a cigarette and passed it to me. The older soldier seemed satisfied I was not injured.

"You hit the ground pretty hard," he said. "You really need to let the medics check you out when we get the all clear."

We stayed there for who knows how long and eventually moved inside the building next to the bunker to see what was going on. This was some sort of MP/Command area and they were on the radios and the hard line trying to figure out what was going on. I sat on a sofa for a while and eventually we were given the all clear. I went back to the CHU where the word was passed that the company was doing a formation to check for casualties. *Great*, I thought. *Let's go stand in a big damn group after catching rockets.* At this point my head was killing me and I felt like I was both deafened and shaky, with a ringing or metallic tone sound to keep me company.

At the formation, I told SPC Byrd what had happened and he kept an eye on me while we waited. Word got back to Snake Doc, and nothing keeps him from a soldier needing medical attention. He pulled me aside and he and another amazing medic, SPC Renee, checked me out. Good news was my ear drums had not burst but I very likely had a concussion. He wanted me to head to the clinic with a medic escort to make sure I did not have a brain injury, which had been causing all sorts of problems for soldiers. As with all information in the Army, once word got around that I was hit, all sorts of misinformation had spread. Word got around that I was either dead in the blast or being medically evacuated to Germany among many others.

...

When we arrived at the clinic the nurse looked at my ID, smiled; and said, "Really? Wow, happy birthday, I guess."

The Doctor checked me out and ordered a few scans, and confirmed that I had a minor concussion. The battalion sergeant major as well as the battalion XO stopped by to check on me. The sergeant major told me to call home and make sure they knew I was ok, because it was possible that I showed up on some casualty list that may have triggered a call to my fiancé and scare the hell out of her. I was also ordered to see a mental health professional, which was amusing to me since that was my civilian occupation. I skipped that appointment. At this point I had a raging headache and exhaustion when the adrenaline dropped off. But I felt glad it was over. I headed to the phones to call Amanda who got really scared, and I had to explain what had happened. I did not envy her the task of letting my family know, since they worried so much about me. If I died in combat, my poor father would never have heard the end of it from my mother, who would have been happier if I had never joined the military.

The next day, I walked to the impact sight where the EOD guys were working and it sobered me up immediately. It was way worse than I remembered. It took me a second to figure out where I was when it hit; the iron cord helped me figure it out. It was right on top of me. The point of impact was about a foot or so dug in and everything in the area, as high as the 16 foot blast walls, had chunks of concrete torn out. The lights on the walls were shredded. We were finding razor sharp shrapnel as far away as two football fields' length away. There was less than a thigh-high concrete divider separating the high parking area from the slightly lower elevation where the rocket detonated. It had divots and chucks all over it from the shrapnel.

There were shrapnel impact marks everywhere and yet I walked away with just a minor concussion. The EOD guy noticed my interest and was more than happy to talk with me about his profession. I told him where I was standing and you could see him do some mental calculations.

"Yep, you should be dog meat, brother," he said around a mouthful of chewing tobacco. "Probably what happened was it hit the low ground here and you were in the exact right spot for it to miss you, and it just hit the bank and concrete. If you were standing anywhere else, that would have been it. I have seen these things take a chunk out of Striker armor and make hamburger out of people. You are one amazingly lucky sumbitch."

The next day my roommate Roberts dug out a piece of shrapnel from the bank and gave it to me, after breaking my balls for a while asking what stuff he could keep of mine if I died. On the way back home, a cool Navy customs guy let me take it home in a plastic case. To this day, I don't play the lottery because I have used up all my luck in a lifetime.

...

This next section is a little hazy on the details; keep in mind I am writing this several years after this took place, with only my journal as a guide. I spoke with several of the other soldiers that were there during this incident, and I think we managed to piece this together pretty well.

The convoy mission was on an usually a long road. We would leave Talil in the evening anywhere from 1800-1900 and roll onto post as late at 0800 in northern bases like Balad; from daylight to daylight. We were stuck behind another convoy in a winding single lane outside the post, with a small village to one side and an Iraqi Army checkpoint on the other.

I was alternating on the radio between the landowner and local command, and shooting the breeze with my soldiers. Somewhere along the line, there was a concern with the local Iraqi Army guys and Sons of Iraq (SOI) at the checkpoint. If I remember correctly, the KBR guys or TCNs said a few of them had approached their vehicles and checked the door. The decision was made that Bulldog and my truck would pull over and put myself and CPL Wallander on the ground while the rest of the convoy slowly made its way inside the post. Driving inside the ASV, you always look for a chance to stretch your legs.

The Sons of Iraq were typically local males from the area that wore reflective vests and were paid by us via the local government to man checkpoints. This basically was paying people we used to fight a living wage to keep things peaceful, in many ways making it in their best interests for things to remain calm. In reality, these were the same Sunni insurgents and Shia militia members that would love to kill Americans given half a chance. It would not have surprised me if they were looking to grab an American contractor and take him God-knows-where to make a decapitation video for YouTube.

Captain Bourne had recently told us how some Iraqi Army tried to detain an American captain, and they ended up drawing down on each other. While you can be respectful, you never trust anyone that is not wearing an American uniform. Iraq's military and police thrived on corruption and split loyalties, and us being there did not change that fact.

On the ground, CPL Wallander and I lit up our smokes and said hello to the Iraqi Army at the checkpoint. There were about six to seven men there and one spoke English very well. He asked me a number of questions. He seemed pretty shady. It seemed like he was smiling at his own inside joke. Bulldog and I talked for a while and kept an eye on the guys. While we were outnumbered, if something were to happen to us the turret gunners would have turned these guys into hamburger. Calculated risks; if they were up to something then it would be harder to do it with us staring right at them.

Before too long, the convoy was headed inside and we loaded back up in our vehicles. Right about then, the radio sounded off.

"Hey Cookie, this is Coop. The civilian convoy leader just said that they are taking small arms fire from the field to our three O'clock. Break. Our gunner said he thought he saw tracers. Over."

"Roger Coop, this is Cookie. I am headed back that way. All units move to see what the hell is going on, over."

"Roger, this is Bulldog. We are headed that way Cookie."

My driver was already headed off road to the right of the convoy between the field and the trucks before I could give the order. A good driver knows what to do. My gunner had the turret whirring, looking for any enemy combatants. I hopped back on the radio to the local command to let them know what was going on and to make sure there were no other friendly elements like patrols or QRF in the area so we would not have a friendly fire incident. Things got confusing very quickly because someone had said over the radio that there was no apparent damage taken.

"Cookie, this is Gonzo," I spoke into the radio. "We don't see anything at the convoy's three o'clock, over."

"Cookie, this is Bulldog. I got a truck headed our way on a little road coming out of the field, I'm going to shut them down and see what is up. Over."

A few moments later, Bulldog sounded off. "Hey Cookie, Bulldog. They are headed off the route back toward the main highway. I'm following. Over."

"Roger, Bulldog. Gonzo, go with him. We are moving the convoy inside. Over."

My driver hit the gas and we were flying toward the rear of the convoy and quickly caught up with Bulldog's truck in pursuit of what looked like a truck with some uniformed Iraqis in the back. Most times like these, it seemed like I had schizophrenia trying to sort out all the voices on the radio and in my own gun truck. My gunner, SPC Roberts, had a night vision scope on the .50 and said there probably wasn't anyone else out there but that Iraqi truck and they probably took some pot shots at the convoy. Roberts had a previous deployment to Iraq with the Marines and was fairly used to uniformed Iraqis taking shots; not a one of us trusted them. My driver was saying that someone could easily have hid out there somewhere. So we were flying after this vehicle, and before too long Cookie jumped on the radio.

"Bulldog, Gonzo, this is Cookie. Come on back. You guys are getting pretty far out there. Over."

At this point the truck had made it to the main route/highway and was headed to another checkpoint marked by a tall concrete column.

"Roger Cookie, this is Bulldog. We are headed back your way."

So what happened really? It's hard to say. One of our trucks definitely took some fire as there were some impact marks on the KBR armor and glass and we had to take pictures. One gun truck crew says they would have noticed the small arms fire, while another was fairly sure it did happen. To this day, I believe some Iraqi Army soldiers took some pot shots at the convoy and then drove away. This was how most things in Iraq went down. Most war movies and stories have clear narratives of how things went down, but in reality, you never quite know what is going on until afterwards; and sometimes not even then. At this point, it was a war of harassment. Most of the casualties we sustained were IEDs and indirect fire. Time and again the Iraqi Police and Army showed us they were corrupt and not to be trusted.

Chapter 11

Typical Convoy & Other Surprises

A good way to understand convoy operations in Iraq is to take you on a mission.

The missions would begin the evening before with a "showdown," where an inspecting NCO or officer would inspect all of your gear, weapons, supplies, and vehicles. Repetition works... We would be staged by our vehicles and the company commander would inspect every aspect of our gear and our trucks, with serious attention to detail. He'd check our lights, our weapons, and make sure our turrets all worked. Captain Bourne had a serious thing about weapons; he used to inspect weapons of his soldiers as they would walk by, which actually helped keep people aware of how clean their rifles were.

My ASV was a problem child; with crappy air conditioning and a serious vacuum and hydraulic leak in the turret, which got "fixed" a dozen times by our mechanics. I finally was able to find civilian contractors in Balad who spent the day fixing the turret. Not only that, but they gave me tens of thousands of dollars in parts to bring back to my unit to get some of our other vehicles up and moving. My XO, Captain Nighthawk, put me in for an award for that one. There were times we could not get new tires because they were being shifted to Afghanistan as combat operations were heating up over there.

If all was well after the showdown, you stowed your gear and worked on whatever maintenance or nonsense task came down from higher command.

...

The next day we would walk to the truck yard, load ammo, and then drive our vehicles to the CHUs to get our overnight gear. Then we'd head to the chow hall around 1700-1800 to eat dinner. Afterwards, we would line up our vehicles by the battalion TOC and wait on the intelligence briefing. Sometimes I sat in on the briefings, where a few lieutenants and captains would let us know where the recent attacks and IEDs occurred, and what else to expect. It really seemed like other convoys were getting hit a hell of a lot more than we were. Maybe we kept better eyes on IEDs, or we just looked like we were paying attention. Around this time I would be issued my communications list of where/how to contact the landowners for the mission.

After the briefing, we would head to a small trucking Forward Operating Base (FOB) called Cedar II where we got our food and beverages, and we met up with the civilian trucks we'd be escorting. We did a minor search of all the Third Country National (TCNs) workers and vehicles. They came from all over the world and we made damn sure that their tires were either in good shape, or they changed them before we left. At this point, we would check our radios and equipment one more time and get into formation. As a tradition, we listened to "Convoy" by Johnny Cash over the radios, then rolled out. We had two lead scouts, then our pace car, followed by about 30-35 civilian big rigs, my vehicle, then another 30-35 vehicles, then finally our command and tail gunner trucks. This made for a line of trucks which spread out for several miles on the road. Coming out of Cedar II, we blocked the roads as we waited to make sure all our vehicles got on the highway together.

Things were pretty calm in the south of Iraq at this point in the war, and the route we rolled did not see too much trouble until later in our deployment. Most of the time we would switch positions in my vehicle—we'd change out gunner, driver, and truck commander positions—until we reached Scania, to reduce fatigue. SPC Roberts was our main gunner and I wanted him fresh for the more dangerous areas of Iraq. But we were all qualified turret gunners as well as drivers, so it helped to switch things up. More often than not, I would be the gunner in the south, which I enjoyed for the most part—except for how uncomfortable the seat was.

Our truck had two main roles in the convoy beyond providing firepower. The first was to relay information from the front trucks of the convoy to the back, because the two elements could not communicate to one another. Second, I was to speak with the landowner units as we left and/or entered their areas. They provided our backup if we needed it, and were a good source of information, like if another convoy found an IED a few miles down the road, if there were known enemy in the area, etc.

As we entered a new area, it would sound something like this:

"Sawgunner X-ray, this is Centuar 26, over."

"Centuar 26, this is X-ray, send it. Over."

"Sawgunner X-ray, this is 26, we are 77 vics [vehicles] and 112 packs [people] at checkpoint Sierra 12. Destination Seitz. Please send SigActs [Significant Actions: IEDs, attacks, etc.]. How copy?"

"Centaur 26, this is X-ray, we copy 77 vics and 112 packs en route to Sietz, SigActs are IED det [detonation] at 11 Alpha at 1530 with some small arms fire. Over."

"Roger Sawgunner X-ray, this is 26. Standing by. [I can still be reached on this channel] Out."

Then, to inform the rest of the Convoy:

"Gonzo to all Centuar Elements, positive communications with landowner. SigActs are IED det at 11 Alpha at 1530 with some small arms fire. Over."

"Gonzo, this is Cookie, roger. Over."

Scania was the halfway point in the mission and the dividing line between north and south Iraq. It was just a fuel station, and toward the end of our deployment we found it was better to carry our own fuel and drive around rather than stop. North of Scania, the chances of running into trouble was far higher. At this point, we would get back in formation and continue the mission north. Rolling north meant it was time to put your game face on. Complex attacks, where there is an IED and small arms fire, were pretty rare because we stomped the hell out of anything they could throw at us. Even better, there was a very low chance of any of their small arms rounds hitting anything important. My ASV alone had both a .50 caliber machine gun and a belt-fed grenade launcher ready to drop accurate short and long range fire in a heartbeat. So the smart move on the enemy's part was to set IEDs to kill Americans while they were out of sight.

I remember one of the mechanics said to me, after we came back from a long mission waiting on EOD to detonate an IED we found, that "the war is pretty much over anyway." Easy to say when you never leave the base. Yet, there was probably some truth to that. The attacks had decreased dramatically since the Surge, but tell that the wounded and killed soldiers we were getting every single day, especially in Sadr City and Mosul.

North of Scania was a small FOB called Kasul at which we stayed a couple of times. The south and a couple of hours north of Scania was mostly open highway and desert. I would say about 3/4s of our missions were to Balad which was by far a much longer and far more dangerous mission. The area between Taji and Balad accounted for a vast majority of the casualties for convoys like us because it was north of Baghdad and chock full of pissed off Sunnis who were much more likely to fight us or drop an IED.

There were many times we found an IED and had to cordon off the area and wait for EOD to come clear the way. It was always a long wait and it was easy to forget how dangerous an IED could be when you would much rather drive around the sucker and get a mission that did not last 16 hours. There were many times we were not sure if it was an IED or not and we would just shoot it to see what would happen. One mission, Captain Bourne was riding with the scout truck and we had stopped for the third time for a possible IED. The captain got out and kicked the damn thing. It turned out to be an empty 155 artillery round but it could have just as easily blown him to Hell. To this day, I'm not sure if that was courage or stupidity.

White Knuckles

We had been running as the second scout for the convoy while Slick and her crew were on their two weeks of leave. My driver was also on leave, so SPC Roberts was the gunner and I drove for this mission, while we had an involuntary fill in in the passenger seat. SSG Mathis was nice enough but did not really fit into any CET, and was very socially awkward. I had already cleared with Cookie that this was my truck, and established that Mathis was there for the ride since he had very little experience. He fell asleep pretty quickly on most missions.

So far it had been a pretty easy road on the way to Taji when we turned the corner and we were right on top of what looked like an obvious IED. I felt my stomach drop, thinking it was just about to blow. If anything was an IED this was. Both scout gun trucks saw it at the same time and screeched to a halt right on top of it.

"Coop, this is Bulldog. Halt the convoy. We may have something here. Gonzo, you see this? Over?"

"Roger Bulldog, let's take a look. Over."

At this point in the deployment, my gunner and I bickered like an old married couple and this mission was no different. We had to do a threat assessment before calling EOD, which would mean we would be stuck in a fairly dangerous stretch of the route before EOD showed up to clear it. I pulled up to park the front left edge of the truck over the possible bomb to get a better look. We were less than five feet away.

"Hey Kritch, pull back and I can look at it with my scope," Roberts said.

"Negative. I can see it way closer from here," I said.

"That's bullshit, the scope will magnify it and has night vision," Roberts fumed.

"Listen asshole, let me look at it first and I will pull back so you can. I am trying to see if that is a wire right there or just a strand of the tarp."

Just then I looked over to see SSG Mathis gripping the handle bar with white knuckles. All the blood had drained from his face and he looked terrified.

"Hey there, Sergeant. Are you alright? You look white as a sheet."

"If that's an IED, shouldn't we be backing off of that thing?" he said.

"Negative Sergeant, we got to clear this thing before bringing the convoy around. If that's the kind of IED I think it is, it's not going to matter much if we are a few feet further away."

We rolled missions about every three to four days, each lasting two to three days, and we had become pretty acclimated to the dangers. It was almost more academic at this point. It's easy to forget how this guy was feeling, as he was not used to this kind of thing. We went back to inspecting the IED and Bulldog put his brighter-than-the-sun light on it and we could see through the outer shell. It appeared hollow.

"Gonzo, this is Bulldog. What do you think? Over."

Roberts and I agreed it was nothing. SSG Mathis relaxed. "This is Gonzo. Looks fine, let's get going. Over."

Pieces of You

We were stuck behind a route clearance team, which are basically either Navy or Army Explosive Ordinance Disposal teams (EOD) who have specialized sensors and equipment and go out every day to search for IEDs. I guarantee there are hundreds of soldiers, myself included, who owe our lives to these guys. That being said, it sucks to be stuck behind them because they move five miles per hour for their equipment to work properly. We halted our convoy as they called back on the landowner frequency that they had a weird heat signature they were investigating. We waited for about an hour, smoking cigarettes and ranking the hotness of various celebrities when I heard laughter on the landowner frequency.

"Centaur 26, this is Seeker 46. Over."

"Seeker 46, this is Centuar. Send it."

"Roger Centuar, this is Seeker. We are going to get moving here pretty soon. Turns out that we found an IED that was detonated accidently up here and the guy who set it is a 50 meter smear. We were trying to figure out what all the other signatures were, turns out it was body heat, we sure the hell aren't picking him up, so they are calling in some Hajis to clean this up. Sorry for the delay. Over."

"Roger, Seeker. This is Centuar. Thanks much. Over."

"Hey Cookie, this is Gonzo. Over."

"Roger, Gonzo. What's up? Are we moving soon? Over."

"Roger, they are rolling out now. Turns out that some Haji went to the Wile E. Coyote school of bomb making and blew himself up. Over."

"Roger, couldn't have happened to a nicer guy, Gonzo." Snake Doc responded.

Lost Cookie

Every now and then, every CET and company screws up. CET Centuar 16 rammed an Iraqi Army truck that drove out in front of them and sent it spinning and injuring a bunch of Iraqi Army soldiers. Wasn't their fault. There was no American taxpayer-funded equipment we could issue to the Iraqis they couldn't ruin in record time, if not outright sell or strip for parts. That being said, I heard that our company and battalion commanders spoke with General David Petraeus about it. Our own screw up was a pretty weird little anomaly.

We were rolling south of Scania, home free, listening to music on the last leg of the mission home. We had been down a gun truck for several weeks because of maintenance issues so we were running five gun trucks with only SSG Sierra/Cookie Monster as the tail gun and command vehicle. My crew and I were arguing about what constituted road music when Slick called out.

"Hey Cookie, this is Slick. Are you kidding me with this? Over."

Silence.

"Hey Gonzo, this is Slick. Cookie may be out of range on my radio, could you call back and see if he can hear you? Over."

"Roger Slick. Cookie, this is Gonzo. Over."

Silence. I felt some anxiety start to creep in. I had my driver pull off to the side of the road and asked my gunner to see if he saw Cookie's truck at the back of the convoy. Maybe his radio had died.

Nothing.

"Hey Slick, this is Gonzo, I can't get him on the radio and my gunner can't see him. Over."

"Roger Gonzo. Hey Coop, this is Slick. Halt the convoy. Over."

"Roger Slick, this is Coop. Halting the convoy. Over."

"Hey, I got a message on the Blue Force Tracker that Cookie's truck died and he is stranded behind us. Bulldog and I are going to drive back and see him, Gonzo move to the rear and Coop hold the front. Over."

"Roger, Slick. This is Coop. We'll hold down the fort. Over."

Turns out that the Mine Resistant Ambushed Protected vehicles (MRAPs) were prone to catastrophic electrical failure and that was what had happened. Their vehicle's electrical literally caught on fire all at once and they were left behind since they were the last vehicle and no one could see them. Stranded in the desert all alone, could have been tragic but ended up being an inconvenience.

Once they figured this out, the scout trucks took off and we waited protecting the convoy while we got the band back together. Before long, I started getting messages from the battle captain (the officer back on base who monitors missions) on the Blue Force Tracker requesting a situation report. The message lag was significant and communications south of Scania were unreliable, so I was getting three increasingly pissed off messages from the battle captain all at once. I forwarded the messages to Slick and then we waited some more. After the first hour, we started getting bored and started stretching our legs outside and checking on the convoy. It was open desert. Nothing was going to sneak up on us, so we took the liberty of shooting our rifles a little at targets we threw out into the sand.

Turns out a friendly convoy had come across Cookie's truck and towed them while shooting us a message on the Blue Force. There wasn't anyone else around to notice it. After a very long mission, we returned to get an ass chewing and it launched an internal investigation. Honestly, the captain that investigated the incident was a decent sort and it did not end up being a witch hunt conducted by bored people with rank like I thought it would. No fault was found; it was a catastrophic and unforeseeable equipment failure. We honestly should have thought to set up the convoy a little better, but live and learn.

Chapter 12

Iraqi Nights

The Cordon

North of Kasul and south of Sietz, we were headed back home on a damn long mission from Balad. We had several unscheduled overnight stops at Taji, then Seitz, due to heavy IED detonations in the area which kept shutting down the routes. We were finally headed home when a convoy ahead of us identified an IED. Of course. We didn't seem to be able to drive for one hour in a direction before we or someone else found yet another IED. I had a substitute driver on this mission and my regular driver, SPC Baldwin, aka Charlie Brown, was the gunner. Cookie called out instructions.

"Cookie to all 26 units, we need to establish a cordon so no one gets by until EOD gets here. They are pretty sure they have something here. Over."

My ASV was in the center of our convoy and we stayed busy watching our right and left sides while the head and rear of the convoy was handled by the scouts and rear gunners. We waited. Watched. And waited some more. It had been a damn long, unpredictable mission and everyone was tired. Then the radio called out.

"Hey Gonzo, some Iraqi Army Humvee just drove right through our cordon and ignored us. SHUT HIM DOWN!"

My driver was way ahead of me and flexed out and hit the gas. We flew right at the Iraqi Army Humvee, not knowing what to expect. The Humvee tried to get around us but our driver adjusted and got right in their way to shut them down. Once they stopped, they tried to get by us again. My driver blocked them. The doors to the Humvee opened and I grabbed my rifle and popped my hatch to get out. I was furious.

"Hey Chuck, watch these assholes."

"You know I got you, Kritch."

Chuck Brown had popped the top of the turret and was up with his M4 so he could provide backup if this got out of hand.

I slid down the front of the truck, my teeth gritted. Two men exited the Humvee, one dressed in the Haji dark digital camouflage, and the other some version of a khaki uniform. While the gunner and a third passenger remained in the vehicle. The soldier in the digital uniform had an AK with a folding stock, pointed at the ground. Mr. Khaki had some odd side arm and was probably an officer. He was drunk; I could smell it, and he swayed when he stood. He was tall with a face like he had just smelled something awful, and had an aggressive posture.

"Do any of ya'll speak English?" I said.

"Yes. Some English. Yes," said the soldier.

"You want to tell me why you ran around our gun trucks when we told you to stop?"

"We have Colonel with us. We go around."

"Sorry, but no. There is an IED up there and we are not letting anyone within 500 meters. It could go off and kill people. You need to stay right here."

At this point, the Iraqi officer took a step forward. I don't think he understood what we were saying, but he was pissed about my tone. I was guessing he was a Sunni, some of whom can come off a little high-horsed since they were in power under Saddam's reign. I looked right at him.

"Are we going to have a problem?" I said, looking right at the drunk.

"No, we go." managed the drunk officer.

"No, you do not. You stay right here." I could feel blood rising into my face, I was getting angry.

"He is Colonel, we go through," the Soldier said. I could tell he wanted to keep the peace.

"And I'm a corporal saying *no*." Not giving an inch.

At this point the colonel got out of the Humvee (that we recently gave them) and spoke with his subordinates for a moment. The drunken officer was obviously trying to press the point and the soldier seemed to be explaining about the danger the IED posed. At this point I crawled on top of my ASV and put on my headset to speak with Cookie to update him. SPC Baldwin was watching the whole mess while smoking a cigarette.

"That one is about to piss me off, Kritch," Baldwin said.

"I hear ya, just keep an eye on them," I said. "Cookie, this is Gonzo. Over."

"This is Cookie, send it. Over"

"This is Gonzo. They want to drive through, I told them no. Can we send them back the way they came so they don't have to sit here with us? Over."

"Roger. You can roll them back this way or they can go around through that access road. Over."

"Roger. Standby. Over."

After I explained their options, they drove the far way around via an access road. We radioed the friendly military forces that direction to give them a heads up. Again, this incident was not that big a deal, but shows how young enlisted guys sometimes have to make decisions way above their experience (and rank) level.

Flat Tire

We were rolling northbound, east of Baghdad late at night and we had just passed through the Widow Maker, which was as well-known spiral ramp notorious for IED fatalities. There is a lot of American blood and blast marks on that blacktop. The previous week we had reports of insurgents throwing armor piercing grenades (RKGs) over the wall and taking pot shots at passing convoys. This was a predominantly Sunni area and the people here were prone to attacking Americans.

As the last of the convoy passed through the Widow Maker, we noticed a large gap in the convoy as a supply truck had pulled off to the right.

We realized the truck had lost a tire in a big way, but we had to keep the rest of the convoy together. Cookie brought the back half of the convoy forward a mile or so up the road and left my gun truck and SSG Garcia's Humvee as security while this scared-looking foreign hired hand from God-knows-where changed out the tire. The highway was surrounded by tall concrete blast walls with rubble and debris all along the highway. Iraq was a country covered in trash in its streets. It was dark tonight, with the constant smoke from God-knows-what always billowing from somewhere, promising us all cancer further down the road.

We were never far from the smell of urine and feces; the Hajis would pull up their long robes and use the bathroom wherever they felt like it and did not use toilet paper. Half a mile back, on the other side of the Widow Maker, was an Iraqi Army checkpoint. You never knew if they were there to help or harm.

Garcia and I were on the ground while my truck was positioned south toward the Widow Maker, and Garcia's truck faced north toward Taji. Our gun trucks were out about 100-150 Meters away, and SSG Garcia walked around his gun truck to get a better view of things. I stayed with the foreign driver as he attempted to change his tire, just to make sure he was doing his job and not wasting our time. These guys spooked real easy.

SSG Garcia had been with the 10th Mountain Division during the battle of Mogadishu. These were the events depicted in the movie *Black Hawk Down*. Hearing stories about being a brand-new medic in one of the bloodiest modern battles was fascinating to me. He talked about casualties stacked four-deep in a canvas Humvee, with 18 killed in action (KIA) and over 80 wounded. They later said over 1,500 Somalis were killed in the fighting, by both sides.

I never stopped moving. It's much harder to hit a constantly moving target, even with everything else going for you. I was surprised how quiet the night was; I could hear 15-ton gun truck engines rumbling nearby in the distance, and the clank of the tools of the TCN as he fumbled with them. I usually had my head filled with traffic from the radios, but this was the actual sound of Baghdad; far away traffic and purring military vehicles.

Then I saw a vehicle approaching. It confused the hell out of me. Normally, the headlights on our gun trucks (other than Humvees) were taller than I am, and the only Humvee with us was SSG Garcia's up front. I stepped back toward some cover; surely my truck would not have allowed some joker to drive right up on us. My blood was up and I was in that odd state where time seemed to slow down, and I was ready for whatever would happen next.

The doors of the Humvee opened and some Iraqi Army soldiers stepped out wearing their dark digital camouflage and silly Mickey Mouse berets. I relaxed just a little bit, but never forgot who they were and where I was.

"Good evening, do you need help from us?" An Iraqi soldier said in quite good English. It never ceased to amaze me how well so many Iraqis could speak our language.

"No, we are doing just fine," I said. "Just a flat tire, we will be on our way soon."

"Hey Kritch, we doing alright?" SSG Garcia had walked up to investigate.

"Roger, Sergeant. We are peachy."

"Ok, thank you. Good night." The Iraqi Soldier said placed his hand over his heart, which was a respectful gesture. They loaded into their Humvee and drove out towards Taji, our lead Humvee calling it up to the rest of the convoy so they would not be surprised or mistake it for us.

Another 20 minutes went by; the TCN had the foreign recovery vehicle helping at this point since they had a hard time getting the damn tire replaced. Cookie was getting impatient, so we were trying to hurry them up. This was not a good place to be. Then I heard a shot ring out.

And it was nearby.

I did not hear a snap or hiss near me, but they were pretty close, probably two or three total. The TCN definitely heard it. I told the TCN to stay down and I scanned the area. Nothing. There was high ground on both sides of the highway, with ragged apartments and concrete balconies everywhere. The Iraqis also do what is called "celebratory fire" where they fired their rifles in the air, because someone got married or other nonsense. Of course these bullets have to come down eventually, and sometimes kill innocent people and children. I ran over to my gun truck and banged on the side door. It took a second, but my gunner's head popped out like Oscar the Grouch.

"I just heard shots, I didn't see anything but let them know up front."

I checked on the TCNs who were almost done now that they had motivation, and jogged over to SSG Garcia's truck.

"Did you hear that?" I said.

"I had my headset on, but you said you heard shots? My gunner thought he heard it too, but didn't see anything."

"Alright, let's get rolling. We have been here way too long."

The TCN was done and I told him to get ready to roll. As I was moving toward my gun truck, I marveled at how beat up these trucks and how they looked like they belonged here. I got to my truck, mounted up, and checked in on the radio.

"Cookie, this is Gonzo. We are headed back towards ya'll. Over."

"Roger, Gonzo. When you get here, we will Charlie Mike. They said you heard some shots? Over."

"Yeah, didn't see anything. Over."

So what happened? Not sure I will ever know, could have been someone taking pot shots or something that had nothing to do with us nearby- we were just outside of Baghdad. There was no shortage of Sunnis who hated Americans and almost everyone had an AK-47. It's frustrating because we had every ability to strike back, but most of the dangers in Iraq vanished as soon as they appeared.

Chapter 13

A Taste of Home & Back to War

15 Days in Texas

In late February, and I was scheduled for 15 days of leave stateside. I was going home, which almost seemed a foreign concept at this point. I had come off of mission and turned in my weapon with our supply sergeant. For about 24 hours, I was walking around Talil unarmed and I did not care for the feeling. I seriously doubted something would happen where I would need it, but not having my rifle by my side gnawed at me. I packed one duffel and one backpack and went to the local Haji Mart to get gifts for my fiancé and family. The next morning, hurry up and wait was in full effect. I went with Sergeant Shoe and Specialist Hopper from 2nd Platoon. We, of course, were stuck in the equivalent of an Air Force waiting room for the better part of 12 hours before we managed to get on board a C-130 headed to Kuwait.

We landed in Ali Al Salem, an air base in Kuwait where we were waited in a large hall, and several hundred of us took the better part of the day to store our armor and helmets in a warehouse and to secure our civilian itineraries. Afterwards we had the better part of a day to kill before wheels up, and I walked around the nice little base. I can't imagine how nice it would be to be stationed there, and one soldier told me he got his combat patch with this deployment. Apparently Kuwait was considered a combat zone. I drank coffee and watched a movie in a massive recreation center. I read a book called *Beautiful Boy* about a father watching his son deal with an addiction to amphetamines. Absolutely worth the read. It puts things in perspective. I would much rather go through this deployment a dozen times than watch my family go through something like that.

Before long, we were up at zero dark thirty with all our gear to fly on a commercial plane to Atlanta, then on to Texas. This trip was a blur in comparison; I watched movies and listened to podcasts counting down the hours until I was back in the great state of Texas. I sat next to a chatty Navy lieutenant who overall was a decent sort, but looked down his nose at me sometimes as if he had to explain "big picture concepts" to me about Iraq. He spoke like someone who had watched a lot of CNN and never spent one hour outside the wire, much less ever in danger. To be clear, I would switch places with him in a heartbeat. Since I lived on missions between bases and IEDS, I'm allowed to be a little cynical and entitled.

We landed in Germany and I bought a piece of the Berlin wall like every other tourist, and got an overpriced cup of coffee and sandwich. I enjoyed a cigarette in the freezing German winter with a bunch of other homesick soldiers and marines. Before long we were headed to Atlanta, killing time with short naps and movies. When we landed, we had to haul ass to get to our next gate and check in. I would be damned if I was going to waste any of my 15 days in an airport. On the last leg I was bumped to first class with another soldier where the steward offered us a drink. So we got beers and short whiskeys. There was another service member who reminded us there was no drinking in uniform, we thanked him for this information, and promptly ignored him. The whiskey helped take the edge off a little.

As we arrived at the glass walkway at Dallas Fort Worth Airport, the crowd below cheered as a dozen soldiers came off the plane. Most places I went in uniform, the people were amazingly gracious. There are days where it's easy for the public to forget what we are doing overseas, but we are there in your lines and at your tables in every airport, always waiting to go home or leave again. I took a small prop plane to my home town where I was thrilled to find that my 15 days would not start until midnight, since it was already early in the morning.

Amanda was there waiting for me, breathtaking as usual. Every time I saw her, she looked so different. I felt like a stranger in my home town. Everything looked exactly the same except for me. I weighed about 175 instead of my usual 200 plus pounds, and my skin was Iraq-sun scorched. I returned to my home to spend time with my future spouse then take the dogs for a walk. The uniform was left where it landed for a few days. It was odd to wear civilian clothes and have no real pressure or responsibilities.

The next day, my friends Jason and Melanie threw me a Mafia-themed party. My wife wore a short leather jacket and did her hair perfectly like a Mafia princess. I wore a track suit with a gold chain. My friends drove in from all over Texas to drink with us and tell lowbrow jokes.

Over those two weeks of leave, my family brought me food all the time, and I must have eaten at a different restaurant almost every day.

Most importantly, I spent time with my fiancé. I know a lot of soldiers who basically got hammered with their buddies most of their leave, or blew all their money on clubs. I wanted a slice of peace, not more chaos. We walked the dogs on long trails at a local park and walked around the lake where we would eventually get married. We even took a short trip to the Metroplex, but before too long it was time for me to go again for the last time. Somehow this time was easier, but this was wearing Amanda out. I didn't really tell her everything that was going on; because I knew it would just make her worry more. This aged us as a couple, and challenged us in a way that nothing else could.

Before long, I was on the plane back to Kuwait. We were back at Ali Al Salem for about three days this time. I was not in a rush; I just burned time and let the clock run down on the deployment. When I landed in Iraq, I walked my gear back to my CHU in the dark. There were 20 weeks left, and I was ready to close them out.

Air Support

We rolled out of Taji headed southbound and only made it about 20 minutes down the road before we were stuck behind several convoys because of an IED. We would all be waiting on EOD at this point. A nearby Mosque blasted its evening call to prayer and there were a bunch of locals milling around, which makes soldiers in a halted convoy feel a bit nervous. We had LT Ortega with us for this mission, and after the first hour of waiting, he dismounted and walked around with several of the other soldiers to keep an eye on things. SPC Roberts had popped the top of the turret and was watching our people on the ground. I would smack the turret cage if I needed him. So I was left on the radio, monitoring the channels and relaying information.

The way my radios were set up, I could listen to up to three channels at the same time through my headset and we had the hard-mounted powered antennas so my radio could reach at least three times further than most. The first channel was always the convoy's internal frequency, the second was the emergency channel for medical evacuations, and the third was for the landowner. I also had access to the frequencies of the other American convoys on the road, which I received at the intelligence briefings. While looking at my Blue Force Tracker's readout, I heard traffic from one of the convoys stuck ahead of us waiting on EOD.

"Wolfpack Xray, this is Road Dog 16. Over."

No response.

"Wolfpack Xray, this is Road Dog 16. Over."

No response.

"Any station, any station. This is Road Dog 16. How Copy? Over."

"Road Dog 16, this is Centuar 26. Reading you Lima Charlie [Loud and Clear], over."

"Centuar 26, this is Road Dog 16. We are trying to contact landowner Wolfpack Xray.   Please Relay. Over."

"Roger Road Dog, prepared to copy. Send your traffic."

"Centuar 26, this is Road Dog 16. We have two to three possible dismounts in an elevated position with possible weapon system at grid coordinates Foxtrot Juliet 123 678. Break. Currently limited due to IED location to respond. Over."

After confirming the message, I reached out the landowner.

"Wolfpack Xray, this is Centuar 26, relaying for Road Dog 16. Prepare to copy. Over."

"Roger Centuar 26, send it. Over."

I relayed the message, word for word, back to the landowner unit.

"Roger, 26. This is Wolfpack. Standby."

I switched back over to update Road Dog 16 and tell him I was standing by.

"Centuar 26, this is Rotor 55. Over." Rotor 55 was the callsign for a helicopter sent to investigate the men spotted by Road Dog.

"Rotor 55, this is Centuar 26. Over."

"Centuar 26, this is Rotor 55 we are airborne, send location of threat. Over."

"Roger 55, this is Centuar. Grid is Foxtrot Juliet 123 678. I have you on Blue Force, will tag location and send to you. Over."

"Roger Centuar, this is Rotor. We got it. Over."

"Road Dog 16, this is Centuar. Be advised. Rotor 55 headed to your location on landowner frequency. Over."

"Roger Centuar, this is Road Dog. Tango Mike [Thanks Much]. Over."

At this point I saw a bunch of friendly elements in the area on my Blue Force Tracker. I ended up getting busy emailing with our command and speaking with my own convoy and the interaction slipped my mind. At some point I sat on the hood of the ASV smoking a cigarette and the LT showed me you could see helicopter rotor static with night vision, even if you could not see or hear the bird itself. I caught some more of the landowner freq's radio traffic. It was an expended ammo report from Rotor 55.

Oh hell, I thought. It could have been nothing, but sure sounded like they found something. Not long after they sent the local Striker patrol for follow up, I could see them circling around to the location ahead of the lead convoy to investigate. Those helicopters are angels on our shoulders, and I was glad to help out when I could.

Chapter 14

The Back 9

Fame

In late June, I was eating chow with Baldwin and some other soldiers when the news came over the television that Michael Jackson had been found dead. Endless bad jokes and worse puns later, we geared up for our mission and left the wire in the evening. Driving through a series of checkpoints southeast of Baghdad and passing one of our other convoys heading south, I played "Thriller" through my gun truck's external PA speaker system. I watched gunners in the other convoy rave dancing with chemical lights as we took verbal shots at each other over the radio. Hilariously, one of the Iraqi Police officers did the zombie "Thriller" dance. It was deeply funny and surreal to see an American artist and weirdo so well-known worldwide.

After we completed our mission several days later, we were pulling security outside of Cedar II and waiting to return to base (RTB). The areas surrounding Talil and Nasiriyah were a flat desert wasteland with only the occasional camel herd or goat farmer. Tiny mud houses, some abandoned and some inhabited, dotted the landscape and highway. Children begged for food or water along the highways while the adults worked to scratch out a desperate living in the middle of an occupation. The kids would sling rocks at us if they did not get what they wanted, or they did it just for the hell of it. There was a large portion of the Iraqi population that was very nomadic and traveled with their wares or animal herds across the region. Baldwin had popped the top of the turret and was smoking a cigarette watching a couple of goat herders nearby. Before long, I heard him laughing while talking to one of them.

"No, I'm not giving you my watch. Not my damn glasses either, Jesus. Hey Kritch, this fucking guy is asking for my gear."

"Maybe he is looking for a sugar daddy," I said.

"Hey Kritch, this guy wants to know if we want to get freaky-deaky with the goats?" Baldwin was laughing full on now.

"Hey man, tell him that is offensive and it depends on the goat…"

I had my driver listen for the radio as I pulled off my headset and popped my hatch to check out the entertainment. One herder had a gap-ridden smile and wore head wrap with a white robe or man dress as we called them. The other wore a similar man dress and was a little cross-eyed, and seemed amused as hell messing with us. The goat herder's next question was very surprising to me.

"Hey, is Michael Jackson dead? Did he die? I hear, yes," the first man said in quite good English.

"Wow, you heard about that, huh? Yep. He died, not sure what happened though."

The man translated this to his brother. Who responded in intelligible Arabic.

"That is sad; we like Michael Jackson."

We eventually gave them some water and American cigarettes and they went about their business. It struck me that a day or so after he died, Michael Jackson was so famous that a goat herder outside of Nasiriyah knew he was dead. That is true fame and a sign that our world was getting smaller by the day.

The Real Enemy

We had begun our right seat/left seat with the unit that was going to replace us. It was very exciting, knowing that we were in the process of coming off mission. As with all things, we were the step child of the Artillery Battalion and while other convoys were being pulled from missions so they could pack their crap, our mission load increased. We had only one day to reset between missions before we were back outside the wire. The incoming unit was compromised of infantry soldiers of the South Carolina National Guard. Just like any unit, they had some squared away soldiers and some truly awful human beings. Their first sergeant was a dangerous combination of lazy and opinionated. Our own first sergeant was trying to keep him from drowning despite his best efforts to sink. I watched some of these young soldiers trying to pull the weapon system off of the ASV turret like a bunch of monkeys making love to a football. They were hilariously offended that I asked Pop Tart, the female gunner, to square them away.

I had already gone out with the ASV crew a few times; my gunner was leading his own gun truck at this point so I had their truck commander, a very small sergeant nicknamed "Squeak" and his gunner, a solid young grunt with a sharp mind and good discipline. We arrived at the staging lanes where I was supposed to just ride along and allow them to run the show. We were only a few weeks from heading back to Kuwait, then on to Fort Bliss in the great state of Texas. I was dropped off at the lanes where the truck was already running late, which was not a great start to your first trip outside the wire on your own. I was smoking a cigarette with Snake Doc when I noticed there was a problem after my truck arrived. The squared away replacement gunner looked worried so we walked over.

"What's up, Squeak?" I asked the sergeant.

"I can't do it, Kritch. I just can't do this," he managed with his head down in a panic state.

"Ok, what's the problem? You have already done this several times, I will be there if you run into a problem but you need to suck it up and get over this."

"I'm sorry, I just can't," he said quietly.

"I get the fear, I was nervous as hell going outside the wire but you get used to it. You are a sergeant with soldiers under your command. You need to be the example; you are a leader. Take minute and get it together. No harm done."

Snake Doc usually had a way with people.

"I may have a tampon in here somewhere that may help you out," he said, looking in his aid bag with a big smile on his face.

"Listen…" Squeak began.

"No, you listen," I snapped. "There is something to when you wear this uniform, it comes with a price and this is your price, man. You are scared; we are all scared at some point. That's part of the game, but when you look back how would you liked to have handled yourself?"

At this point, I felt it was a problem and more than just nerves, so I headed to Captain Bourne to get his two cents because I couldn't exactly excuse this guy from a mission. Snake Doc stayed behind to talk with the young NCO. Captain Bourne was nearby, talking with the replacement company commander.

"Hey, Kritch. What's up?"

"Sir, can we talk for a second? We may have a problem."

As we approached, a few other soldiers had gathered around, trying to get this young sergeant squared way.

"Hey sergeant, what's the problem?" Captain Bourne said.

"I can't go sir, I'm sorry," he said meekly.

"Why? Is something wrong with your weapon or truck?"

"No sir, I have a kid being born soon and I need to be there for them…" he trailed off.

"Oh. I see. You're a pussy," Captain Bourne said, said looking truly irritated. "You need to unfuck yourself and get ready to roll out. You have already rolled on several missions already. What was the difference then?"

"Crihfield made me feel safe…" he said choking back tears. I could hear Snake Doc laughing to himself already.

Captain Bourne stomped off to drag his captain over to the situation. The captain spoke for a few minutes, then I saw this young sergeant grab his weapon and gear and walk back toward the housing area.

"He is having a hard time with this, we will move him to the TOC and switch someone out later," their captain said.

"That's the wrong fucking answer!" Bourne said. "Is that what we do when someone doesn't want to go to war today? You have got to be fucking kidding me! What do you do next time this happens? Ask another company to carry your weight?"

My convoy commander asked me to roll as the truck commander for this mission. The look of disgust from his gunner was priceless. He warned us this was far from over and they would handle this when they got back.

A few days later on the same mission, we were rolling back towards Talil, right next to Kasul, on a pretty uneventful mission. Bulldog came over the net.

"Hey Coop, this is Bulldog. Halt the Convoy. Over."

"Roger, Bulldog. Halting Convoy. Over."

"Hey Cookie, this is Bulldog. I got an Iraqi Policeman saying there is an IED up ahead over here. Over."

"Roger. Everyone look around their vehicles for other IEDs. Gonzo, get ahold of Landowner and get EOD out here."

It was odd. The IED was pretty obvious. There was both Iraqi Police and Iraqi Army present in greater numbers than we were used to seeing. Bulldog said they were being a little squirrelly. I called in EOD from the landowners and we waited, watched, and established a cordon (perimeter) like we always did. Strangely, the Iraqi version of EOD showed up pretty quickly, which we had never seen before, and they had all different manner of explosives already with them. And they were just waiting at the back of our convoy.

Something was wrong.

After about two hours, American EOD showed up and confirmed our suspicions.

"Centuar 26, this is Bomber. Hey, are those Iraqi Police still back there with you?"

"Roger, Bomber 46, they are back here with us. We have eyes on them. What's up? Over."

"Listen, Centuar. Those Police were the ones trying to hide the IED; it looks like you surprised them when you rolled up. There were two IEDs, a hoax (fake) and a real one. Keep them there with you, we are going to request that the landowner at Kasul send QRF backup so we can detain them. First, we are going to try and detonate this IED. Over."

"Roger, Bomber. Hey Centaurs, watch them and try not to let them in on what is going on." Cookie said.

I later heard that SPC Roberts told them that we were so grateful for their help we were going to send out money as reward and they should stay to get it. Very damn clever. I had also later heard that SPC King was getting really pissed and the Haji cops could tell. They were a wrong sudden move away from being shot down where they stood. I was in the center of the convoy in eyeshot of EOD and Bulldog, but my blood was boiling mad. Just then Cookie came over the radio.

"Gonzo, this is Cookie! A civilian truck just got past us and is headed your way, shut them down!"

"Roger, Cookie," I said.

We were already moving and we saw this large Haji big rig rolling right down the road at us. It was covered in brightly colored fringe and pictures as the Iraqis like. We went straight at him. I could hear the turret behind me draw down on the truck, which is pretty damn scary to have twin grenade launcher and a .50 Cal barrel point at you. This could well have been a vehicle borne IED, and with the size of the truck, would have made one hell of a crater. Often we have to go with our gut, and my gut said this guy was just an idiot trying to get around yet another American traffic jam. Our sirens and horns were blaring as we rolled our 15 ton gun truck straight at him. He got the message and pulled off to the side. He looked terrified. My gunner had popped his hatch and I was almost halfway out of mine to tell this guy to shut down his engine when...

BOOM!

It's a sound you feel in your bones and guts; it shook the truck and went right through my hearing protection as if it were not there. For an instant, I knew I was hit with an IED or that the truck exploded. That awful moment when you know you just might be dead. The Haji driver looked as terrified and surprised as the rest of us. What seemed like forever, but was probably just a few seconds, went by until it registered what actually happened.

EOD detonated the IED and it shook the world. Chasing this truck down brought us way closer to the IED, although probably still a "safe" distance, and it scared the hell out of us all. The Haji driver thought we shot at him and was asking my gunner not to kill him, and that he was sorry. We explained it was the "boomballa" (IED/Bomb), which they all understood, and he seemed relieved. We all laughed nervously as we lit our smokes.

Then the nonsense machine started back up. Word came down from landowner that we were not to detain the Iraqi Army and Police involved. The all-knowing Fobbit Brass of Kasul had asked the Iraqi authorities who, shock of all shocks, said no. We were at a stupid point in the war where we were letting the Iraqi authorities call the shots and police themselves, and we were just a "partner." EOD wanted to use us and QRF to drag these bastards to Kasul and test for explosive residue, then send them on a trip to Gitmo, a task for which we were all more than happy to assist.

EOD gave us the all clear and we rolled the convoy back home. I have a vivid memory of hatred for those Iraqis. As we rolled out, they ran down to where we detonated the IED and threw the debris in the air, and acted like children in a pile of autumn leaves. They got away with it. If this were still the invasion, they would have been bleeding in the sand. I felt rage and I felt homicidal. I can't tell you these same Iraqis didn't set the next IED, which took one of us out. I can't tell you that they didn't lob a rocket or mortar into Kasul later in the week and send a folded American flag to some wife or mother. Hell of a thing to want someone dead that badly, then be told no. They took our money, wore our taxpayer-funded uniforms, and tried to kill us. And we did nothing about it.

This is a piece of my war.

Red Air

When a sandstorm blew in, it looked like a thousand foot wall of sand rolling toward you. On mission, you could barely see 30 meters in front of you and the sand would roll in waves across the blacktop of the routes like water. If we were about to leave for a mission, we would be told to stand by for up to seven to eight hours before a mission would be pushed until the next day. If we were already on the mission we would have to stop at the closest FOB until it cleared up because it meant that the medical evacuation choppers could not get to you. And it was aptly named—the sky would turn red as blood with sand so dense you could feel yourself walking through the particles in the air. You would constantly have grit in your teeth, nose, and eyes while waiting to even begin what would be a 12-16 hour mission. Hurry up and wait.

The Last Mission

Time was counting down for us; we had already moved back into tents and were setting up to go home in a few weeks. Things were not smooth at all. The South Carolina National Guard was failing to take the lead on their missions. Our NCOs and a few of our soldiers were still rolling with these guys well past when we should have been packing up to head to Kuwait. The number of IEDs increased dramatically and we started finding them on every mission.

The convoy was hit outside of Scania and they failed to take the lead, forcing Cookie and Slick to hold their hands through the whole process. In fact, Slick and Cookie were still on mission with these jokers when we were just about to fly out.

A month or so prior, our battalion took its first casualties. Two Soldiers from Bravo 3/124 Calvary were seriously injured. An Explosively Formed Projectile IED (the most deadly) hit the scout vehicles of their convoy. The super-heated molten copper, traveling faster than a bullet, entered just behind the truck commander and hit the driver and gunner. They were all sent to Germany for medical treatment. There had been casualties around us before; amputations and deaths listed in every single intelligence briefing I attended. I felt we had been due for a while. Every landowner unit told me about a fresh IED or American death. There was something about the thought of being dead and not seeing it coming that is terrifying. We could have been rolling just like we had done a hundred times before, then: lights out.

Our replacements had serious trouble maintaining contact with the various landowner units, and I stopped helping them at one point. Sink or swim. They were late to every mission and did not seem to grasp the seriousness of the process. I had a sick feeling that they would get someone killed once we left. There were a few of the soldiers that were squared away, but overall they had some hard lessons to learn about leadership and organization.

I was the gunner for my ASV's last mission. They had replaced Squeak with another soft spoken, country-fried NCO from their headquarters. His southern drawl was so damn thick that the landowner didn't understand him half the time so their Convoy Commander had to also handle communications.

On one mission, we were rolling south and halted to top off our fuel when I felt a weight lift off my shoulders. I had popped the top of my turret and was smoking a cigarette, looking at the lights of the distant city and the open desert's clear sky. My mission was done. This had been such a long and brutal process, but here I was standing at the end of it all. I just listened to the night air and diesel engines, safe and sound behind my .50 caliber and grenade launcher in the same part of the world that Alexander the Great and Moses walked; a Marlborough in Mesopotamia. I felt the history of this war and my place in it. Coming home, it was going to be hard to explain this whole process. That it was not about the danger or depravation, it was about the displacement. Pulled from a life to follow orders and strain to do the best with what you have. I knew that in a month I would be home for good. This was a concept that just seemed odd in the middle of this open desert, some 5,000 miles away.

As we crossed the last bridge, we cheered as we fired our flares into the sky and weapons into the sand.

We were going home.

Chapter 15

The Road Home: Hurry Up and Wait (Again)

Everyone Gets a Trophy

After my last mission, I was pulled to the TOC by LT Spears and LT Ortega to write up awards for our soldiers. I am a fairly good writer, but the Army has a very specific way they write awards. The ones that had already been submitted were rejected by battalion and we only had a short time to fix and resubmit them before the award ceremony. After a damn long mission, I spent the rest of the night typing awards for damn near every soldier in my platoon, and even helped with some from 2nd Platoon and Headquarters. Captain Nighthawk went out and got us all coffee and food since we were working through the night. There were several soldiers that I refused to write up awards for. For the most part we had some of the best soldiers, but we also had some that were not only a waste of oxygen but were a damn liability. People had carried their weight for them the whole deployment. Sorry, sir. Not going to do it. LT Ortega understood and handled it.

It was a mad scramble. My roommate had volunteered to extend his tour with an incoming infantry unit, and moved into a new CHU within the week. Mixed information filtered down from command about what must be done before we headed to Kuwait. We worked hard to bargain with supply to issue him an M4 since he was still carrying the M249 SAW. I had spent four to five hours in line at the post office to mail home stuff I could not carry home and did not want to leave. Afterwards, we had a medal ceremony, at which my eyes almost rolled out of my head completely. We were lined up and everyone was issued at least an Army Commendation Medal.

Everyone received an award; even the soldiers who had lost rank from Article 15s or worked in the damn chow hall. Even more offensive, everyone over the rank of E7 and lieutenant on up received a Bronze Star. Even the Fobbits who seldom, if ever, went outside of the wire received a Bronze Star, if they had the rank. To me, the Bronze Star meant something. One soldier in our company received a Bronze Star from his last deployment by pulling his CO out of a burning Humvee while under fire. That is how you should be awarded a Bronze Star, not because you showed up to a war in your Army pants. The final insult was that everyone in the company was awarded the Combat Action Badge. Again, this included everyone employed full time as a Fobbit working in the chow hall or at a sandwich shop and seldom, if ever, was in the slightest hint of danger. I was disgusted.

Then the nonsense got even deeper as an argument began over what combat patches we were authorized to wear. It was like children fighting over Legos. According to regulations, we were authorized quite a few, since our battalion was separate from our brigade and we were subordinate to: 7th Sustainment, 287th Sustainment, 1st Calvary 1st Brigade "Long Knife," and 3rd Expeditionary Sustainment Command. Captain Bourne said we were only authorized 3rd Expeditionary, 287th Sustainment, and 36th Infantry. I could give a crap less, although I agreed with him, and typically wore one of those three. Mostly I wore the 287th Sustainment since their sergeant major gave me his patch after we spoke outside of their TOC one day.

...

I sat on a bench by the Chapel with Captain Nighthawk and smoked a cigarette. LT Ortega told me that CPT Nighthawk submitted me for a medal for bringing all the supplies home to fix our truck fleet. The award got flushed by the battalion commander. I thanked him for the thought, and was glad.

"Doesn't matter what they were awarded, they know who they are and what they did here, and we do too," CPT Nighthawk said.

"Sir, for that wisdom; I hereby award you the Silver Star."

...

I had been selected with our operations NCO, SFC Aaron, and a few others to fly out a few days earlier as Advanced Party to square away the details for the rest of the company to join us in Kuwait. We cleaned our tents out, walked our heavy equipment to the local air strip, and lined our gear up outside, leaving us with only our weapons and a carry-on bag. Endless delays and cigarettes later, we waited over 16 hours before being told we would not be leaving that day or the next. We found a place to crash and managed to kill another 10 hours the next day in a recreation area until we were finally loaded into a C-130 and landed in Kuwait. We stayed longer than we thought we would, before being loaded through a series of Navy Customs stations where we were shook down a dozen times. A Navy E-6 got a little big for his britches, and yelled at us for making too much noise while waiting for yet another step in the process. I thought SFC Aaron was going to beat him to death right in front of us.

I am never the guy who acts all high and mighty because I served in a combat position. In many ways, it was the luck of the draw. When we started out, we were going to be guarding gates and FOB towers as well as the damn Post Exchange. I remember running into an NCO I held a lot of respect for in Bravo Company who ended up guarding the Post Exchange in Taji. He simply hated every day of the deployment and would switch with me in a heartbeat and done a great job. That being said, it irritated the hell out of me when Fobbits would give us grief. This little Navy puke wanted us to be quiet in order to make his easy little air conditioned job easier. We resented people who told us we could not enter the chow hall because we were too filthy from coming off mission and needed to shower first. These people did not understand we were sometimes coming off missions that lasted 24 hours with nothing but water, energy drinks, and snack bars to keep us going.

This time in Kuwait was probably the first time I felt a lot of the pressure lift off of me from the deployment. We had to unload some trucks and do a few minor jobs here and there, but overall we had four days or so by ourselves with no needless drama. I read books on my cot and drank a million cups of coffee and used the internet for more than five minutes at a time. I perused the local Haji markets and bought gifts for the family and friends back home. It was peaceful for a short time.

When the rest of the company landed we drove them to the tents and started the long process of trying to get our unit back home. The rest of our brigade was already home in Texas. Apparently the brigade commander made a big deal about "bringing all his people home," seemingly unaware we were still in combat operations at the time.

Before long, we were wheels up on the freedom bird home. It was surreal and a little hard to wrap our minds around. It was over. We landed at Fort Bliss, in El Paso Texas, early in the morning. A cheer went up as the wheels touched down. We were greeted by an Army band playing, and our generals shaking our hands as we came down the stairs. Then we were basically mugged for our equipment, and I handed off my weapon and signed it away before getting a bunch of injections from the medics. I no longer carried a weapon and it was a very weird feeling; I felt very exposed. We loaded into a large room. I just got a sandwich and coffee and sat down next to SPC Byrd and CPL Stone to talk about football and our plans now that we were stateside. As a bonus surprise, my buddy Tom who was injured and pulled off the deployment was there to help us out.

We loaded up on some buses and everyone and their dogs were glued to cell phones as we traveled to barracks waiting for us in New Mexico. Once at the barracks, we all looked around, surprised, when we heard the Arabic calls to prayer over the loud speaker. It was supposed to mimic the conditions on the ground for deploying Air Force and Navy personnel.

The next week went by in a series of briefings and equipment turn in while we killed time by taking the local shuttle back to Fort Bliss to watch movies and shop at an actual shopping center. Deploying units are supposed to have 90 days of leave following a deployment to get back situated before returning to full active duty (or drill, depending on the branch).

We were given orders to report to a reintegration conference in the Metroplex, and that anyone who did not attend would be Absent

Without Leave (AWOL), which is a serious criminal offense. I lost my cool and actually argued with Captain Bourne about this. I, like almost everyone else, had made plans. Mine happened to be my wedding, and I would not be attending some damn Army conference. He told me straight-faced then I would be AWOL. So be it then. Captain Nighthawk backed me up and said that was bull and there was no way he would let that happen.

We conducted medical evaluations and the soon-to-be-deploying 72nd Brigade Combat Team was looking for volunteers to fill their ranks. There were also recruiters from the new Ranger and Special Forces battalions looking to snatch people right up as they came home from deployment, which is a pretty smart move considering many of the soldiers did not know how they would earn a living after this was over. This is also when we found out that the slots in our home company had been filled while we were deployed. This was shocking news in that many of us that were from the original medical company before it was adapted for convoy operations now *did not have a home unit.*

What was worse, we could not even promote our veteran soldiers until we had a valid slot that most of these new soldiers filled. The officers, including Captain Bourne, informed everyone loudly and publicly that deployed soldiers would have first slots regardless of who was currently occupying them. While we had been gone, recruiters rushed to fill our positions, and now there were not enough positions to go around. Unit manning procedures were, by far, the most frustrating part of the Army National Guard as it affected every other part of a soldier's career. We were all so tired of the constant administrative headaches that many great soldiers decided to go Reserve, Active Duty, or get out. Specialists Dayton and Cooper joined a Reserve Drill Sergeant Unit and were promoted almost immediately.

The following summer, at my last Annual Training, I was finally promoted to sergeant, along with sergeant Stone, by the new squared-away Commander of Charlie Company, who cut through the administrative nonsense and finally pinned our rank. It was also backdated somewhat to make up for the severe delay of processing. I moved to the Headquarters Company and wasted time until my enlistment was finally up, right at the same time we were scheduled to train up for Afghanistan. They tried to hard sell me another six year enlistment with a signing bonus and "guaranteed" promotion to staff sergeant, but I had walked that path before and I was ready to go.

The rest of my life was waiting for me.

Normal, or Something Like it.

CPL Wallander and I landed in our home town at the small municipal airport. As I walked off the plane, no one was standing there. I turned the corner and saw my gorgeous fiancé, with her long dark hair and an adorable sun dress. I felt a joy I had not felt in so long because I was home for good. We would not have to go through the loss of separation again. It took me a while to register that the rest of my family was there—as well as my friends with signs and balloons. My friend Melanie took professional photos of the moment. I said my goodbyes to family and friends, and my brother Brent offered to take home my duffel bags that would not arrive for another hour.

I was home. There really are no words for this feeling.

The first few weeks were amazing and everyone I knew lined up to take me out to eat or visit with me. Amanda and I stayed busy getting ready for our wedding, which happened less than one month later. We were married overlooking the lake we had walked around so many times before I deployed. It was one of the best days of my life. After our honeymoon in Maui, we eventually bought our own home with the help of a very low interest VA home loan, and we both returned to school to build a life together.

This is the end of the story of my war in Iraq, but the not the end of my story. This next section may hopefully give both civilians, veterans, and those who may one day wear the uniform some perspective on how we changed with the war experience.

Chapter 16

The Wounds You Don't See

At Fort Sam Houston, I was a young soldier in AIT who came upon a training dummy in the thick woods during a field training exercise. My squad pulled security while I placed tourniquets and pressure bandages on the obvious wounds.

The training NCO walked up and said, "He is dead."

"What? Why sergeant? What did I do wrong? I used the tourniquet, bandaged the wound, and placed the IV on the first stick. Why is he dead?" I asked, tired, frustrated, and covered in fake blood, dirt, and sweat.

"It's not the wounds you saw, it's the ones you did not see that killed him," he said.

...

Life moved on. I returned to school for three semesters and got my Social Work license and worked as a program therapist for a private psychiatric/substance abuse hospital, which contracted with the military to provide service for Active and Reserve members. I spent the next few years completing my Master's Degree in Clinical Social Work and graduated with a 4.0 GPA from the University of Texas at Arlington, which had a top notch Administrative and Military focus. When the final clinical licensure is completed, I plan to return to the military as a medical officer in the Reserves to see if I can serve my country in a way other than kicking IEDs to see if they work.

I worked with hundreds of soldiers, airmen, sailors, and marines with severe addiction and mental health diagnoses such as depression, post-traumatic stress disorder, traumatic brain injury, and both substance abuse and dependence issues primarily involving alcohol and pain killers. I spent countless hours in group therapy and individual counseling, and working with spouses and families to give each the best chance of success that I could offer. There were successes and many more that slipped further away despite everything we could do to help. Overall, I loved my work and was satisfied of where I was in life. Normalcy had started to settle in again.

The world reminded us how violent it can be on November 5th, 2009. I had just got out of group therapy at a military treatment program. I was sitting near the nurse's station, writing my notes as my patients took a break by the television in a lounge until the next session. The news came over one of the 24 hour news networks that there was an active shooter at Fort Hood. I stopped what I was doing and walked over to the lounge with my soldiers and watched the news pouring in. Many of my patients were from Fort Hood, and were terrified for their friends and families; we pulled out every phone we could to let them call home. We cancelled the next group and just watched the news; a group of men so acclimated to violence overseas had to watch helplessly as it literally struck home.

One of the worst things was that the former Major Nidal Hasan was a psychiatrist who had a working relationship with our facility. He very likely referred many of our patients for inpatient treatment. He probably had deep emotional issues and was easily manipulated and radicalized by those that wish our country harm. I doubt he was "insane," whatever that means. He made a choice to kill his fellow soldiers and to insult the country, which gave him so much. I have always maintained that leaders need to watch their subordinates closely for red flags and alarming behaviors and intervene before it becomes a tragedy. The news detailed many alarming statements and interactions Hasan reportedly had which should have been a bright neon sign screaming DANGER. From Nidal Hasan to Columbine High School, people will find twisted reasons to visit violence on others. We need to be prepared and vigilant.

...

I was painting the hallway in my new home with my wife Amanda. She has an amazing sense of humor and we laughing hysterically about something when my phone rang.

"Hello," I said, somewhat still laughing.

"Hey Kritch, its Roberts."

"Hey brother, long time. How have you been?"

"I'm good, we are doing ok. I have some bad news for you…"

"Hang on one second…" I gave Amanda a look, concern crossed her face, and then I stepped out to our new back yard.

"Ok, send it. What happened?" I was getting a smoke ready; I knew by his tone what this was.

"Mathews is dead, he killed himself," he said, point blank.

"Jesus, what happened?" I lit the smoke and took a deep drag, saddened but not surprised.

"Not entirely sure, something about getting into some legal trouble and an argument with his girlfriend, and then I guess he overdosed or something."

"I'm sorry to hear that, I appreciate you telling me. Does everyone else know?"

"Yeah, I've let most of us know but I have not got ahold of Slick or Bulldog yet."

"Ok, I'll give them a call, thanks again."

We talked for a while longer about his kids, his spouse, and his upcoming plans. It was good to hear from him and life tended to get in the way of calling or going to see old Army buddies as much as we would like. When the call ended, I called SGT Wallander (Bulldog) and SGT Dickenson (Slick) and let them know what had happened. Wallander was an older veteran and had tried to talk with the kid when he were overseas about the road he was on, since it was one he had walked himself; but being that young means you are stuck in your worldview and you have it all figured out. Finally I called Captain Nighthawk and let him know what was going on, as he was also someone also who tried to talk some sense into Mathews. He took it well and we discussed how this was becoming an epidemic in the Army.

When all the calls were over, I sat in the back yard for a while longer, just processing the news. I had been told when former patients had taken their lives and it was the same feeling. No matter how long ago they had been patients, it boiled down to a simple question: is there something else I could have done? The answer was probably nothing, which is somehow worse.

I was deeply sad. Mathews was very young and stubborn and would never get the chance to grow out of that phase. Mathews and I were not friends; it might have been simpler if we had been. I did not dislike the kid, but I was his NCO and he pretty much stayed in trouble with every person in his chain of command. It was no secret that he struggled with addiction; he spoke with almost everyone about it and sought help several times. He often fought with authority; he was a hot head and lost his temper and discipline in a heartbeat. And he was not alone. There are thousands of young soldiers like Mathews in the Army walking the same deadly line every day.

Disorder

Disorder. It's an ugly word. You never hear the word "disorder" and think of positive things. We sling it around and label soldiers with every diagnosis that we can get our hands on. Post-Traumatic Stress Disorder is not something any commander or potential employer wants to see in a briefing or application. While I did not escape without some baggage, which we will discuss later, I did not have PTSD. Once it is stamped on you, it's very difficult to scrub off. In one of my returning medical reviews, I offhandedly told a registered nurse that I had seen a therapist for a few sessions. No big deal, nothing in particular. Really just some anger, adjustment, and figuring some things out. Every soldier must sort through it; I just chose to accept the help when it was offered.

Two months later, my readiness NCO told me (while I was running a firing range for soldiers) that I had a P3 medical profile (high severity, non-deployable) for psychiatric reasons. It turns out that nurse called some physician who never even spoke with me but he diagnosed me with Post Traumatic Stress Disorder. In my line of work, I was very familiar with the symptoms, and I did not fit the bill. It took the better part of my last year in the Army to submit to evaluations and out-processing to remove it. One soldier had the balls to tell me I ought to keep the diagnosis and get some VA disability money for it. All this time I could not promote or change units until it was handled.

So what are we teaching soldiers by subjecting them to this? Over and over again, I taught suicide prevention briefings, telling young soldiers to seek help and tell someone when they are struggling. When the Army does instead is punish them and limit their careers.

As the years went on, the suicides increased dramatically. The rates of depression and substance abuse skyrocketed. The media was constantly pointing at the trend and the Pentagon fumbled to find an answer to the rising tide. The VA was flooded and unable to handle a fraction of the load in a reasonable time. Often, soldiers would wait weeks or more to see someone one time, then be prescribed an antidepressant and a follow up appointment that probably wouldn't actually happen.

Good luck. Thanks for your service.

Everything is a Spectrum

The most important thing I ever learned about mental health was that everything was a spectrum, or a broad range of symptoms and severity. Symptoms can vary in intensity from minor to severe over time. Someone can be diabetic and take a pill every day to control it, or they need an insulin pump and 24-hour daily supervision in order to survive. Both people are diabetic, but the severity is very different.

The same applies to depression. Minor depression may mean someone feels sad and takes a little more effort to get through the day, while major depression may result in someone wanting to or attempting to take his or her own life. Both people are depressed, but require very different interventions. Time is also a factor. Someone may have minor depression at first and gradually become severely depressed, or someone may be severely depressed, but with treatment and medication, move along the spectrum to minor depression.

There were ingrained changes in me, but most faded with time. Others will probably always be there to some extent. I did not do well with public places and too many people. I needed to sit being able to see the door and the majority of the people around me. While this is a cliché, I found it to be true. If my back was turned I could not focus on the conversation, and my anxiety and blood pressure shot up the whole time. I watched people, closely and sometimes noticeably. Why does this guy look nervous? Why are his hands always in his pockets? I saw threats and looked for patterns. When people would drive aggressively, my whole body would react in rage. I watched all aspects of traffic. Who was driving? How many in the car? What was on the side of the road? I would change lanes needlessly to avoid being close to something in a ditch or too near a vehicle that was driving in an odd way. One night, I was driving to my house and someone was on their roof for whatever reason. I swerved and hit the gas; I was immediately triggered to react to the threat. I felt the adrenaline first and felt silly afterwards. I looked in alleyways and studied pedestrians.

My aggression was very high. One night, someone threw a brick and a bottle at the outside of my house. It sounded like someone kicking in my window. I was outside in an instant in the middle of winter in my boxers with a Glock 23 pistol; I wanted to kill the threat. I walked onto the sidewalk and checked the alley. I saw the glass and brick and my mind was racing; calculating. It was not until I was inside that I realized I was a mostly naked man in the street with a gun.

During one thunderstorm, I thought we were being shelled. My unconscious mind figured I was in Balad and it all blurred until I was awake and able to piece it together. I didn't react, just like I didn't in Balad. I just looked out my window, my mind expecting to see the ground rise up as the shells landed.

The worst example: a coworker at a hospital I worked with was speaking to me in a demeaning and offensive way and I almost lost it. I snarled like a dog and had visions of horrific violence as my body screamed for me to react. I left the room suddenly feeling rage and shame. It was the first time I had almost lost control, ever. It was scary. My engine idle was set much higher and I had to adjust. It got much better with time; some things will always be different. You can't really say when a cucumber put in brine becomes a pickle, but it will never be a cucumber again. This is my new reality.

So how do I not have PTSD again? Because a diagnosis is nothing more than a grouping of symptoms along a spectrum with a group of people to make it easier to treat and research. Nothing more. If I had to be slapped with a diagnosis, it would be Adjustment

Disorder. It is loosely defined as a clinically significant reaction or overreaction to stressors out of proportion, which impair the functioning of the patient. Am I any better with this fancy description? Nope, but it lets a doctor or clinician feel that they understand how to treat me better.

With a supportive home environment and no problems with money or substances, things got much better for me. While I still have some problems, I was able to rely on those close to me and I knew it would pass eventually.

Personal Wars

Soldiers were dying every day, and not from combat. According to the National Institute of Health and countless articles in the media, a service member was killing themselves every day, and a veteran every single hour of the day. We were losing more uniformed Americans from suicide than from al Qaeda. Divorce rates were skyrocketing along with domestic violence. Substance abuse and alcoholism filled the military mental health clinics and VA facilities far beyond capacity.

Why?

Post Traumatic Stress Disorder: The easy answer. The first thing people think every time. Why did he go on a shooting spree? Must be PTSD. The fact is that many veterans do suffer from PTSD and related trauma/stress disorders. PTSD is loosely defined as exposure to a traumatic experience, either personally or from someone close to you, and development of symptoms which negatively intrude on your life. This overwhelms your mind and floods you with fear and adrenaline. It could be the person witnessing the bomb, or the person picking up the bodies afterwards. It's a sexual violation, years of abuse, or the loss of someone which devastated you. It's an ice pick in your brain you can't ignore and a trigger you can't control. It fires you like a bullet and you are always waiting for the next impact. It's hard to ignore, and you dream and think about it all the time. Sometimes it's so vivid you feel like it's happening all over again. You avoid things that trigger it: crowds, people, talking about it, watching movies about it. It makes you depressed; it crushes your confidence and weighs you down with guilt. You are irritable, and can't think straight for months, years, or the rest of your life.

The fact is, according to the studies cited on InterventionStrategies.com, less than 15% of service members who take their own lives were involved in actual combat, and less than half were actually deployed to a combat theater. There are many ways to experience trauma outside of combat, and there is a clear indication that PTSD is a large risk factor for suicide.

Substance Abuse/Dependence: Our engines are always running and the only way to sleep or relax is with a drink or with a few pills. Before you know it, you are in it. Just a drink in the morning to take the edge of the hangover from the third blackout drunk of the week, because CPL Snuffy is getting married or whatever other reason. The Army is a drinking culture. After drill and when we get home. After Annual Training and coming home from overseas. Everyone wants to buy you a beer. Fact is: it's part of the game to get promoted. If you want the promotion, you had better get some face time at the bar or NCO club. You need more than to be qualified, and most of the time you don't even need that; you need to be liked. It does not matter how competent you are. If the higher command doesn't like you as a person than it will take a lot longer to make rank. The good old boy network is alive and well, and the drinking buddy avoids the court martial while the whistle blower is buried. *Sergeant Smith couldn't have taken advantage of the young drunk private, he is a nice guy who BBQs with me on the weekends.*

Pain killers for blown shoulders and shredded knees are taken by the handful and passed around to friends. I worked with soldiers missing limbs hopelessly addicted to pain killers because the alternative is crushing, unrelenting pain for the rest of their lives. They lose their kids, wives, and careers while they do anything for that next bottle of pills. Wives would smuggle booze and pills to husbands in rehab because the very nature of substance abuse is manipulation and control. When they lose it all, depression sets in and death seems like the only way to stop the cycle. The alternative is sobriety, which is in your face every second of every day, knowing that feeling better is a phone call or short drive away.

Al Anon, to me, is one of the most important organizations a family member can get involved with if a loved one is suffering. It saves lives. If you have a loved one struggling with alcohol or addiction, the only way to help them is to arm yourself with information and emotional strength, which are both found in the fortress of Al Anon.

Money: I very rarely have ever seen a soldier in real distress without money being at least part of the problem, if not the main issue. A brand new private straight out of Basic Training starts at $1531.50 monthly with benefits. You may also receive other money such as Basic Allowance of Housing or deployment Hazardous Duty pay which can bump up your income somewhat.

Overall, if you divide 1531 by 160 hours you get $9.57 hourly, which may not sound too bad to someone right out of high school, but let's dig a little deeper. When you are new to the Army, you will NEVER get a 40 hour work week. I have damn near done 40 hours in one drill weekend before. You are at PT at probably 0430 in the morning and you report to your station at 0800, and the day ends when higher tells you it ends. Let's be generous and say you are working 55 hours per week. (Trust me, it can be 130 or more "in the field.") That $1531 is now $6.95 per hour while you are getting beaten like a sled dog.

That is far less than minimum wage for arguably one of the most difficult jobs in our country. As a soldier, you are required to be a varsity athlete and possess at a minimum the equivalent of an associate's degree from your job training. Most soldiers in their first years of service qualify for food stamps. Take a second and absorb that fact. Every year insurance premiums go up, and the quality of the care provided goes down. Many programs and benefits like the Base Commissary where you can make your dollar go further are on the chopping block, which will lead to less access to child care. Now imagine you have a sick child or one with special needs, and imagine not being good with money. Imagine yourself using the predatory payday loan places and car lots that prey on young stupid soldiers. Now imagine getting a divorce, which is far more likely than not in the Army, and paying child support. This can be an unbelievable stressor and you can think you will never dig yourself out of the debt. Your car is repossessed and you can barely pay for the bare necessities when you are working in a high-stress environment day in and out.

I can't tell you how many hospitalization cases started with "I couldn't find a job when I got home." Reserve and Guard guys like me are on our own a few weeks after we get home. I had to fight to get my job back at my hospital because the CEO said my job no longer existed. Others were not so lucky, and I had people trying to go back to Iraq or Afghanistan as soon as they could just so they could provide for their families with tax-free money and hazard pay. The pressure is immense and contributes to every other problem on the table. Together, these problems can make a situation seem very hopeless.

Depression: Depression is common not only to soldiers, but to almost every human that has ever walked the earth. We have periods of grief, sadness, and just hopelessness from time to time, just in the normal course of life. Let's see how that looks for a soldier.

A. I wake up feeling sad or empty every single day, like a puppet walking through my life.
B. I used to play pool and some guitar with some of the guys, but I just can't bring myself to show up anymore.
C. I can't stop eating. I'm overweight and falling behind on my PT test and getting yelled at all day. No matter how I try, I always end up binging on crap then feeling awful for the rest of the day because I am so weak.
D. I can't tell you the last time I slept through the night, I catch a few hours here and there, but never more than three to four. A few months back I slept as soon as I got home until PT formation the next day, but I still woke up exhausted.
E. Everyone says I look like a zombie because I'm always just staring into space; I just zone out and can't focus.
F. The LT is on my case for being a moron again, I couldn't remember where I set the clipboard and Sergeant Davis smoked me until my arms wouldn't work. I can't do anything right as hard as I try.
G. I held my pistol in my lap and really thought about it last night. It will be nice to just rest. I talked with SPC Jenkins about what the afterlife was like since he is so smart but I don't know what I will do yet.

We know that a sense of belonging is crucial in preventing suicide and some studies indicate that the risk of suicide increases following disciplinary action such as an Article 15 punishment or court martial. The shame, loss of rank, and money can have a profound effect on your self-esteem and life. Unlike civilian jobs, you are in for the course of your enlistment. If you hate your chain of command or don't like going to work every day then it can seem like there is no end in sight. As an NCO or officer, it's your job to protect the welfare of those in your command both on and off the clock. If you notice something, or your soldier is not fitting in or being unfairly singled out, it's your job to correct them and provide support as well as to make sure their head is screwed on straight. Anyone can become overwhelmed, so make sure you are having a real conversation with your friends or subordinates every month, and ask questions about their mental health.

Marriage/Domestic Conflict: To many soldiers, the family is a great resource to help manage the burdens of military life. When relationships unravel at home, the stress can push many toward depression, substance abuse, and suicidal thoughts or actions. Imagine coming home from a daily threat to your life and finding out that your spouse has been sleeping with someone you know, while you were overseas, and while your children were in the home. Not only that, when you confront the man she was sleeping with; you are arrested by Military Police or local police for domestic violence or assault. Even if you keep your cool and she moves out, she is entitled to your money. She will also more than likely get at least partial, if not full, custody of your children because you are away so much for training or deployments.

Many soldiers I know faced this exact problem. Some had their bank accounts completely cleaned out while the spouse neglected payments on cars and maxed out credit cards. They came home to debt and foreclosure. Even more common is the young soldier "in love" with their "soul mate" who leaves them or cheats. They don't have the perspective of age to know that this is not that big a deal in the grand scheme of things, and that likely they will have trouble remembering her name in a few years. These are major factors as many of those studied for suicidal thoughts or actions have some level of domestic conflict. This is a major red flag if you see this in a fellow soldier or loved one.

Chemistry: People are afraid of many things: heights, spiders, and public speaking to name a few. While some people are simply afraid of these things, some people have a phobia. A phobia is an irrational, paralyzing, or exaggerated reactionary fear of certain things. Someone scared of snakes will run out of the room if they see one, while someone with a phobia will leave their children and break a window to get out at all costs.

The one thing that causes the same irrational reaction in a vast majority of people is violence. The only people that can function when exposed to death and violence are a small fraction: those who are sociopathic or mentally ill, and people (like soldiers, medical professionals, or first responders) that are conditioned for it. Most people, if you walk in a room and fire bullets in the ceiling, will either freeze or stampede like cattle. It's a fight or flight response, wherein your body is flooded with adrenaline and stress hormones. This chemical flood makes you stronger with more acute senses, but at the cost of fine motor control and both coordination and rational thought.

Your ancestors, all the way to the dawn of time, survived because of the fight or flight response. When they saw a tiger in the forest, they survived because they ran faster than someone else or they froze and were not noticed or considered a threat. Many parents or friends have survivor's guilt from reacting irrationally (when they were not capable of acting rationally) due to the primary fear of violence. Not only that, when your body hits a certain point, you will release your bowels. Not because you are a coward, because that is what your body is designed to do. Read the accounts in World War II of where every man would have messed their pants after a shelling and then laugh about it.

The reason that soldiers, cops, and other occupations don't always react in this dangerous, irrational way is that we are conditioned for it throughout our training. We are used to the tiger. The first thing you are exposed to in Basic Training is fear and stress. You are constantly dealing with stress and being forced to function automatically to certain environments and situations where the vast majority of people cannot cope whatsoever.

Simply put, we react the same way: with adrenaline and stress hormones, but we are not overwhelmed by it. After a hundred times of successfully hitting the tiger with a club in training, when a real tiger shows up, our bodies react automatically with a club. There is a cost to this. The resting heart and adrenaline rate of veterans is higher than the resting rate of normal civilians. We are always looking for the tiger, which takes its toll on our bodies, our ability to sleep, and our neurochemistry.

I can give you a pill, which will make you completely irrational or "insane" for several hours. Does that make you irrational or "insane?" No. It means your brain does not have the supplies to function appropriately. Imagine your brain is a car engine. It does not matter how much you yell at it to start up, or threaten it, or give it money; it won't start without the spark plugs. It does not matter how much motivation you have if you lack the supplies. That's where medication can come in and give you the tools to get the engine started again. Therapy is where you fine tune the engine once it is going. Medicine and mental rehabilitation are not signs of weakness; you would never slap insulin out of a diabetic's hands. Yet if someone takes antidepressants or anxiety medication, they are considered weak.

Weak is knowing something is wrong and not doing anything about it.

...

There is no one thing you can point to as the cause of the dramatic rise in suicide in the military. Our forces are under a strain unlike we have ever known, as far as the pace of deployments. All of these things I mentioned, and plenty of things I have not, all blend together to overwhelm and drive our finest to the ultimate poor decision. The military is not to blame for everything. There are plenty of soldiers who had deep emotional and mental health problems long before they swore the oath of service. Plenty of soldiers use mental health services as a "get out of trouble free" card, causing the chain of command to resent treatment or stigmatize those who have problems or a breakdown. I feel that a minor change on the company level of allowing squad and team leaders to conduct a basic depression screening monthly may prevent a large number of these needless deaths. I further feel that leaders becoming educated about this topic will also reduce the stigma and increase performance at the unit level.

R. Morgan Crihfield

Denouement

This book represents an honest look at my deployment in Iraq and it is my hope that this gives future readers insight into the reality on the ground, the nature of conflict, and the challenges we face as the wars draw to a close. When the final boots touch ground back home and the curtains are drawn on the Iraq and Afghanistan conflicts, we will have to face the challenges of a new age of veterans after America's longest wars. Already, our government draws down the military and cuts the benefits of thousands of wounded men and women who will never be allowed to forget the wars, whose injuries and anxieties will remind them of what they went through.

I ask you, the reader, to support organizations such as the War Writer's Campaign who are helping our veterans heal by telling our stories; the Iraq and Afghanistan Veterans of America who are on the front lines and in the offices of law and policy makers every day saying simply "We are watching, and will hold you accountable." If you want to make a real difference, don't buy a bumper sticker; donate to these organizations.

A portion of the proceeds of this work will go toward the IAVA and the War Writer's Campaign and the amazing work they do. By purchasing this work you are already supporting veterans fighting for veterans.

Thank you.

Morgan.

R. Morgan Crihfield

About the Author

Sergeant R. Morgan Crihfield is a combat veteran who served in Operation Iraqi Freedom with the Texas Army National Guard. He is a graduate of Midwestern State University with degrees in Psychology and Social work as well as a Master of Science Social Work from the University of Texas at Arlington. He currently works as a Therapist specializing in military and veteran's affairs in north Texas where he lives with his wife, children, and lazy Labradors. Twitter: @SergeantofGuard

Mission

To *promote social change surrounding veterans issues through written awareness.*

Vision

The War Writers' Campaign aims to maintain a long-term and historic platform that facilitates the consolidated efforts of service members and veterans to promote mental therapy through the literary word. Its continued purpose of affecting advocacy and assistance will shape and direct the programs of best in class veterans organizations for years to come.

The War Writers' Campaign, Inc. helps veterans in the following ways:

Assist veterans in telling their own story

Engage them where they are in the power of therapy through communication

Empower the next greatest generation of veterans through written publications that generate royalties, create awareness for change, and provide a platform for altruistic giving in the veteran space

Cultivate impact for tangible advocacy – 100% of proceeds from published works go directly back to best in class veterans programs

R. Morgan Crihfield

IRAQ AND AFGHANISTAN
VETERANS OF AMERICA

The War Writers' Campaign is proud to partner with Iraq and Afghanistan Veterans of America (IAVA).

Through our partnership, The Campaign is not only able to support the historical platform for veteran story; we are supporting best-in-class programs that improve the lives of veterans, their families, and our community. The War Writers' Campaign is able to bring together the voices of our Nation's heroes and leverage them for advocacy in the veteran space.

100% of all proceeds support the combined partnership programs of The Campaign and IAVA.

Iraq and Afghanistan Veterans of America (IAVA) is the first and largest nonprofit, nonpartisan organization for new veterans, with over 200,000 Member Veterans and supporters nationwide. IAVA is a 21st Century veterans' organization dedicated to standing with the 2.4 million veterans of Iraq and Afghanistan from their first day home through the rest of their lives.

Founded in 2004 by an Iraq veteran, their mission is to improve the lives of Iraq and Afghanistan veterans and their families. IAVA strives to build an empowered generation of veterans who provide sustainable leadership for our country and their local communities. They work toward this vision through programs in four key impact areas: supporting new veterans in Health, Education, Employment and building a lasting Community for vets and their families (HEEC).

IAVA creates impact in these critical areas through assistance to vets and their families, raising awareness about issues facing our community and advocating for supportive policy from the federal to the local level.

R. Morgan Crihfield

Learn more about IAVA by visiting their website: IAVA.org

Made in the USA
Lexington, KY
11 June 2015